I CLOSED MY EYES AS THE THIRD TOUCHED my hand, and I tried to picture the black sandy beach with the sea of light gently lapping at its shores. *It's me. Do you remember me? I helped you on Epo-5. We worked together there, and I'm hoping we can work together again.*

Something sharp pierced my hand, then I felt something else pierce the middle of my back. I could feel every move the Third made as it dug through my skin and spread inside me. I opened my eyes. "Remember. Wait. Give us a chance."

Who knows what Risa had expected to see, but her eyes were wide, and her face had turned pale.

"Give us a chance," I whispered one more time as my world slowly went dark.

THE CELESTIAL LIGHT

THE THREE-FOLD SUNS

Book 5

by

ELIZABETH KNOLLSTON

ISBN Paperback: 978-1-959159-10-0
ISBN Ebook: 978-1-959159-11-7

Cover Art and Interior Design © Elizabeth Knollston
Editing by Red Adept Editing Services

Published by Lewis Bros. Press
PO Box 261
Larned, KS 67550

www.elizabethknollston.com

for everyone who is a daydreamer
don't stop
let your imagination run wild

1

Decisions and Zips

I stared at the plate of elegantly arranged food. Sauteed flower grass stems were paired with thinly sliced pieces of roasted kiol fowl and a thin glaze of spearberry jam. Miles and Cain were silently eating, while I simply couldn't find the appetite. Cain cast me a concerned look but kept silent. Over the ensuing weeks since the events on Epo-5, both Miles and Cain had tried to tempt me with outlandish creations from the chef, but most only turned my stomach sour.

The Master Glipglow had been running a series of tests and reached a conclusion. The modified smart-bots the Star Eaters had provided Miles to infect me with had begun the process of rewriting my DNA. Despite the bots having been replaced by the Third, the process hadn't stopped. This wasn't like the temporary modifications I'd used to try to sneak onto Dar in order to snag a heart stone, but a nonreversible reconstruction of the basic parts of who I was. More than that, the Glipglow home world had given the master permission to share their database of information with Dr. Kell and the other specialists Miles had brought in. They'd all come to the same inevitable conclusion: what the Star Eaters had done was permanently changing me. What they couldn't agree on, though, was what those changes might manifest down the road.

That was really spectacular news, but there was even more.

Yilmaz remained tucked away in the hab-unit Miles had set up for her, and I'd steered clear of that entire deck. Miles had visited her several times, trying to confirm her theories or trip her up in a series of lies—nobody was better suited than another master of manipulation. I knew Cain had visited Yilmaz as well, but so far, he'd refused to talk to me about it. All I knew was that both he and Yilmaz had received medical attention afterward.

"If you'll excuse me," I said and pushed my chair back. When Cain stood, I shook my head. "No, I need some time alone. To think."

"Perhaps you should at least take a bite before you go," Miles said. "The chef has experimented with the spearberry jam. I know he's looking for feedback."

"That was a poor attempt, Miles," I said.

He'd been getting sneaky, trying to get me to eat. But I obliged the man and took a small bite of the meat. The initial burst of flavor was sweet then turned to a mild sourness.

"Not for me, I think," I said. "But tell the chef I appreciate his willingness to try new things."

Miles frowned. "You really should—"

"I can grab a nutrient pack if need be."

"You said those tasted like zips," Cain said, setting down his fork.

<Don't start. I'm not in the mood.>

<You haven't been in the mood for almost two weeks. You need to eat something a bit more substantial. Even Dr. Kell has raised some concerns.>

<Going behind my back, are you?> I meant that to sound a little playful, but all I felt was annoyance. "Look, you two. I appreciate the concern, but I'll eat when I'm hungry. Right now, I need to go for a walk." And without waiting for further discussion, I left.

When the door closed behind me, I sighed. But the anxiety that had taken up permanent residence in my chest didn't loosen, not one iota.

I paced the decks of the *Samaritan*. We'd transferred back to that ship in order to work with Lio and Dr. Kell. Miles had sent the *Snapdragon* off on some top secret mission he refused to share with me. I let him have his secrets—for the moment.

He'd wanted Ochoa to go with the *Snapdragon*, but she argued her way into staying with us, for which I was grateful. She was a good woman and someone I believed I could trust. That was still a challenge, but Cain agreed with me. Miles was maybe ninety percent trustworthy. I dinged his rating because we still didn't know what he'd promised the commandant when their forces teamed up to fight Lucas and his Sun Worshipers. And Cain was still biased toward the woman after what had happened on the *Justus*. I couldn't blame him one bit. I was a tad bit biased too.

That was one reason I couldn't get rid of my damned anxiety. I was second guessing myself all over the place. I'd listened to the Third and the Star Eaters and had believed they'd been asking for my help. Well, that wasn't technically wrong. They had needed help in re-sorting their connections to each other and the Path Makers. But I hadn't stopped to consider why they'd needed help. My disgust at how everyone else seemed to only want to use them for their own gain had blinded me, not to mention the conflicting emotions over my pops and Lucas.

I'd believed I could rise above them and do something good with everything that had happened. I wasn't like my family or the Sun Worshipers. I wasn't trying for domination or power or any of that junk. I'd thought I could be the one Orion who would be better. *Vain and stupid and foolish and… just dumb.*

By allowing my biases toward my family to cloud my judgment and perception of what had happened, maybe I was now responsible for something far more dangerous. That was the proverbial storm cloud hanging over me. Yilmaz certainly believed I was, and I thought Miles did too, not that he was blaming me. For Jupiter's sake, if any blame was for sale, Miles should've been the first one in line. He'd tricked me on Epsilon's Station with those stupid smart-bots.

My thoughts continued to cycle back and forth, and I wasn't paying any attention to where I was wandering. When I surfaced out of my misery, I realized I'd wandered down into the lowest decks of the *Samaritan*. The one I was on was used primarily for large-scale storage:

spare parts, supplies, and no doubt, a treasure trove of Miles's many obsessions.

Curious and really needing to focus on something else, I took a look. Nothing down there was top secret, after all. And if it was, then they should've keyed in biometric locks on the cargo bay doors.

The first cargo bay was a well-organized repository of spare parts, just as I'd thought. Replicators were great and were used the majority of the time, but any ship worth its salt carried the essentials in case the replicators failed. I meandered down the aisles, recognizing a handful of items stamped with the Confore logo. When nothing wild or exciting jumped out at me, I left that cargo bay and headed to the next one.

It was also unlocked, and I slipped into an expanse of quiet darkness. For a moment, I didn't activate the lights but stood there, letting the doors shut behind me, and I pretended I was once more lost in the tunnels of Epo-5, not as an adult but as a kid. *What would've happened if I'd really died? If the Third hadn't brought me back to life? What would Pops have done? And why had the Third chosen me, of all people?*

We'd all dug into the ancient texts and myths of the worlds we knew Pops had visited, and for good measure, I added the worlds Dr. Ashter had focused heavily on. That was a wormhole topic right there. In the horrible chaos of Epo-5, no one knew what had happened to Dr. Ashter, and Yilmaz was keeping her lips sealed. For several nights, I couldn't help but conjure up multiple gruesome scenarios, including a few where he'd cackled like an old-school villain, twirled his mustache, flapped his cape, and fled into the darkness.

Right. Back to what we know and can act on. All our research confirmed the theory that the Star Eaters—I couldn't think of them any other way now, not after they'd used me—and the Third had been trying for centuries to find the right biological species to use as a bridge in order to repair the damage that had been done. *When they'd what? Traveled here from another galaxy?* Even after everything that had transpired, even that idea was a bit much for me to wrap my head around. The idea of traveling outside of the Milky Way was a dream discussed in jute-store novels. Scientists could theoretically debate about the possibility, but no species in the known worlds had or was developing that kind of technology.

But I didn't know if the Star Eaters wanting to go home was really a bad thing. I certainly didn't think so, but Yilmaz did. She believed the Star Eaters would live up to their name and destroy our part of the galaxy in order to return to their own. And that was a bad thing, partly because I couldn't get rid of my blasted ego. I didn't want the Orion name caught in the middle of yet another scandal—or massacre. Truly, I wasn't sure anything was salvageable at the moment.

Provided I believe Yilmaz's story.

Everyone had come to their own set of conclusions. And I had mine. Decisions had been made. I was just procrastinating, and I knew it.

I lay down on the cool metal flooring and imagined I was slowly being devoured by a black hole. Memories flashed before me, and I pictured each one slowly fading then crumbling into the dark. Pops hadn't been who I'd thought, not even close. Lucas—*Well, I should have known, but still…* My brother was a mass murderer and a crazed fanatic. I recalled all my years as a child, moving from one planet to another, believing Pops was studying the great mysteries of xenology, when all he'd been doing was working for the Sun Worshipers and Mrs. Gol. Even the hard-to-reach memory of my mom was tainted. After so many years—and I'd been so young—I could barely picture her face. Pops had married her on purpose. *Had he really loved her?* I still wanted to believe it, but after all I'd learned, I couldn't figure out what the basis for love between them might've been.

He might've shown affection in wanting to ensure I had a normal life. But if I'd told him what had happened to me on Epo-5, my gut told me he would've squeezed everything he could've out of me.

The door opened, and a small line of light fell over me before quickly vanishing.

<I thought I told you I wanted to be alone.>

Something heavy landed on my chest. I reached up and, as soon as I touched it, knew what it was.

"You said you'd eat one. So here it is," Cain said as he sat down next to me.

"Spoilsport," I muttered.

<This time, I'm not taking no for an answer.>

First, I still hated being told what to do. And second, all I wanted was to wallow in my misery a bit longer. One doesn't simply learn the ugly truth of their family and get up the next day or week or month or lifetime, all zip-a-dee-doo and ready to go.

I grabbed the zip and threw it off into the darkness, hearing a satisfying smack as it splattered against something.

Another one landed on my stomach. I took it and threw it too.

When the third appeared, I grabbed it but sat up. "Geez. How many of these did you bring?"

"And why do you think I'd tell you that?"

I couldn't help it. I laughed. "Fine. I'll take a bite."

"No. You'll eat it. Or I'll make you eat it."

Cain's mission had been successful—somewhat. My mood lifted temporarily, and I leaned into him. "I bet you can't make me."

<Really? You want to take that bet?>

I did. I really did. But my stomach chose the wrong time to let off a rather loud rumble of annoyance. "Fine," I muttered. I ripped open the zip and chewed in silent petulance.

"Lio wants to talk with us. Seems we're at the go-or-no-go zone."

I swallowed and took another bite. *The decision. The one they want me to reaffirm.* The known worlds were teetering on the brink of all-out chaos. Miles had done everything he could to prove we'd defeated Lucas, but the Jumjul had walked away dissatisfied. Everyone was holding their collective breath over what the Jumjul High Court would decide. Also, the Eeri had declared their allegiance to the Jumjul in this whole mess.

"You know we'll follow you wherever we need to go," Cain said softly.

"Why?" I all but exploded. "For Jupiter's sake, why? I don't think my decisions have led us to anything great or grand or glorious. It seems like I keep falling into the same trap, being a tool for someone else's nefarious schemes."

"I thought you liked jute-store stories. True-crime dramas?" Cain asked.

"What?" I said.

"How many times does the hero or detective have to make wrong turns in order to find the right one?"

"Stop being philosophical. I don't think my brain can handle it," I muttered.

"Of course you can," Cain said and put an arm around me to pull me tight.

I'd felt so confident after Dar, so sure that we would figure everything out on Epo-5 and everything would be over with. "But what if my choice leads to another disaster? More lives lost?"

"Then we keep pushing forward until we reach the end. We find the conclusion."

"Is that some IGJ agent training claptrap?" I asked then stiffened, realizing what I'd said.

Cain shrugged. "Sure. Probably. But it's true."

It was. I just wished it wasn't.

2

A Friendly Bit of Advice

When we stepped into Lio's office, chaos greeted us. Ochoa and Miles were yelling at each other while Lio talked with one out of the three guards watching Yilmaz. Cain bristled at the sight of the woman, and I reached out to place a restraining hand on his arm as rage poured out of him.

<There are witnesses here. If you were going to… destroy the woman, you should've done it before this.>

My admonishment was enough to help him gain a shred of control, enough that he backed himself up into the opposite corner and glared at Yilmaz.

"What's going on?" I asked Lio, ignoring Miles and Ochoa. Judging from their flailing arms, I wouldn't have been able to get a word in edgewise.

"Just keep her secure," Lio ordered, and the guard saluted. Then Lio turned toward me. "Miles took it upon himself to include Yilmaz in our meeting. Ochoa isn't happy."

"That's putting it mildly," I said.

Lio's mixed ancestry betrayed him as his fur was

standing on end where it wasn't being held back by his uniform.

"Yes. Well. I've learned that it's better to let her finish her fights on her own than to get involved. Here, look at this." Lio motioned me over to his desk, where he brought up a screen. "I'm assuming you're familiar with a standard military oriented mapping system?"

I nodded. "Confore tech. Top of the line."

Every government had their own way of displaying their forces and anything they deemed a threat. But Confore's programming made changing the display a breeze. So while the individual markers might've been unfamiliar, I recognized the setup. I reached out and touched a purple triangle. A small info box popped up next to my finger.

Eeri. Scout class. Verification enabled.

Next, I touched a cluster of blue squares.

Old Earth military fleet. Class unknown. Verification enabled.

After that was a round, orange indicator.

Jumjul. Destroyer class. Verification pending.

"So we're not getting together to celebrate someone's birthday, are we?" I said.

"No. I had the chef hold back the cake," Lio commented.

I about had a heart attack. "Jokes?"

He shrugged. "Why not? It's better to laugh in the face of impending death than shake hands with it."

I held up a hand. "I'll stop you there. Thanks, I have had my quota of philosophy today. I think I'd rather have had the cake."

"That can be arranged," Lio said, a small quirk of amusement playing on his lips.

I turned my attention back to the screen. "So, if not a birthday party, then what's the occasion?"

"From the intel we've been able to gather, the emperor has gone on the offense, a complete suicide run," Lio snarled. "A waste of lives and resources."

Fudge nuggets and a whole bucket of scuttle crabs. No way did Old Earth have the military capability to stand up to the Jumjul, let alone the Jumjul *and* the Eeri. *What is the emperor playing at?*

"Captain, we should regard this meeting as confidential," Ochoa said, interrupting us.

That was a little disappointing. I was rather enjoying the light-hearted side of Lio. And after the zip, a slice of cake sounded perfect.

"It is," Lio said, returning to full-on captain mode, "which is why I agree with Ochoa. I don't believe Yilmaz should be present."

"Wrong," Miles argued. "We need intel. And she's got it."

"Truthful intel or just more lies and misdirection?" Ochoa asked and crossed her arms tightly against her chest.

"Both. All intel is useful, even the misdirection, because then you know what they don't want you to be looking at," Miles replied. "I'd have thought that was intelligence training 101."

Since Lio was sucked into the argument, I turned my attention to Yilmaz, who, unnervingly, was watching me. She looked tired. Her hair had multiple flyaways, dark circles sagged under her eyes, and her skin had a slightly yellow tinge to it. *Good.* After the suffering she'd caused us, I didn't mind seeing her suffer a bit as well. But the thought caused a rush of guilt at my own heartlessness and the reminder of how "Orion" my feelings made me sound.

I blinked and almost chickened out of our little stare down. But I decided I wouldn't back down. Instead, I walked up to her. "So."

"So," she replied.

"What is it about you that Miles thinks makes you so important? Withholding valuable information? Access to resources he doesn't have but wants? Blackmail?"

Yilmaz smirked.

There she is. The slimy eel.

"Why don't you tell me?" she asked.

I'm not sure what it was—perhaps the potent mixture of Cain's quiet rage, the agitation of the argument behind me, or the feelings of failure and depression—but one or all three caused me to snap. Not in an arm-waving, jumping-up-and-down lunatic style, but a very calm, very focused sense of detachment.

The guards were doing their job, make no mistake. They were focused on Yilmaz and making sure she didn't get up to any funny business. What they didn't count on was one of us going off script.

I reached out and snatched the gun from the nearest guard's holster. I was sure he would later receive a dressing down at having his weapon poorly secured. *Pity.* I pressed the muzzle underneath Yilmaz's chin, and the room went quiet.

"I'd like a straight answer," I said.

"You won't, you know."

"Oh?" I quirked up an eyebrow. "And why is that?"

"Because you've still got a shred of decency left. After dealing with the worst of the worst in my career, I can tell."

"Really," I drawled. "Because it didn't feel that way on the *Justus*. When you were torturing Cain and trying to figure out what I knew."

"I apologize for the oversight there. But I had been working under the assumption that one Orion was like the other. Not to mention the fact our little heart-to-hearts followed your brother breaking into the IGJ and stealing the weapon."

"And so what's changed your mind?" I asked. My finger moved to touch the trigger, and I pressed the muzzle a little harder against her skin. She sat up a little taller but didn't flinch.

"Your heart's blood," Yilmaz said.

<Don't do this.>

"Explain to me, exactly, why we should go to the Eeri. Then I'll decide if I'm my pops, my brother, or just little old me," I said.

Yilmaz maintained eye contact, and I caught a brief twitch of indecision in her left eye.

"As we've already discussed, your father sought the Eeri for a reason. If you allow me to make the initial request, that will be a smart move, considering the Jumjul are in the mix now. I've dealt with both species, enough to have built a tenuous relationship, and right now, we can't risk tipping the scales any further, considering their mistrust of what's been going on.

Besides, the Eeri will have information you need to clean up your little mess."

I leaned forward. "You sound pretty confident. Tell me, how do you know if they've got what I'm looking for? Because if you already have the answer, then I'll give you to the count of five to spill it, or else…"

<Mahia, this isn't—>

<Cain, let me handle this.> I sensed him slowly creeping forward. *<Back off. And tell the others to do so as well.>* He stopped but didn't respond, except for a rather potent mixture of agitation and concern.

"One… two…"

Yilmaz said nothing but pursed her lips and stared at me.

I slid my finger over the trigger. "Three… four…" And my muscles tensed as I had to decide. "Fi—"

"The Eeri are secretive, which should come as no surprise, given the historic trade negotiations they've agreed to. But because I am from a lineage of Gate-keepers, there were meetings and data I was privy to, enough to rouse my suspicions, and I dug deeper into the Sun Worshipers and the Star Eaters. Enough to know the danger the Star Eaters posed. But what your father sought, I don't know. And if I did, I certainly wouldn't be here. I would've finished with this whole mess years ago," Yilmaz said.

I relaxed my arm, let my finger slide back to the side of the trigger, and took a deep breath then slowly exhaled. *Extremely lucky.* I wasn't sure if I was talking about myself or Yilmaz.

"I want everything you have. All the files, the information from the Gatekeepers. All of it. Understand?"

Yilmaz nodded and leaned back in her chair. "You'll have it as soon as I'm granted access to a computer."

I handed the gun back to the guard, who was blushing a brilliant crimson, and turned to Miles. "You'll make that happen. Now. I want that information."

He gave me a tense nod.

"Good. As soon as you get it, send it over to me. I also want a copy sent to Sam. Let the ship sort through the information and match references from other data sources."

"I'll see to it personally," Lio quietly assured me.

"Lio, Cain said we were at the go-or-no-go zone. Is that correct?"

He nodded and glanced down at the screen embedded in his desk. "Yes. We will cross over into Eeri territory within the hour. If we're going to proceed, we need to signal them."

"Work with Yilmaz on that. Let's see if she's telling us the truth about having contacts with the Eeri government," I ordered. "When it's done, let me know."

I brushed past Miles and left the office. Then I marched down the hall and turned into the first empty room. It turned out to be one of the conference rooms. A temptation ran through me to scream and to throw a few chairs around, but the moment I stepped into the dimly lit room, I placed my hands against the cool glass of a screen tabletop and leaned forward. *What in Jupiter was that? What am I becoming?*

Cain had, of course, followed me, and when he quietly

slipped into the room, I threw myself at him and buried my head in his chest. He instantly wrapped his arms around me and pulled me close.

<*I'm sorry,*> I thought. <*I don't know what's gotten into me. I shouldn't have reacted like that with Yilmaz. I really am no better than they were.*>

Cain tightened his grip and rested his cheek against my head. <*A little latitude can be given, considering everything you've been through. And that woman has that effect on people.*>

<*But it doesn't excuse what—*>

<*You're too hard on yourself. No one is perfect. A hard lesson I've had to learn and still struggle with.*>

I pulled back and looked up at him. "Is everyone suddenly becoming philosophical around here?"

"We may have attended a recent seminar," Cain said with a deadpan expression.

I burst out laughing and lightly tapped him on an arm. "Saturn's rings. Sorry I missed it, then. Bet it was a snooze fest."

"The worst."

<*I don't know what I would've done if I hadn't met you. Thank you.*>

Cain leaned forward and gave me a kiss, a very reassuring kiss. *Blow me out of an airlock.*

"If the two of you are finished..." Ochoa coughed, standing in the doorway.

"We are," I sighed as I pulled back.

"Then, if I might have a word?" Ochoa asked. "Cain, she'll catch up with you a bit later."

Cain gave Ochoa a curt nod and one last look at me. <*Together. We'll do this together. Remember that.*>

<*I will.*> At least I would try.

Ochoa waited until Cain was out of earshot. "Yilmaz is many things, but what you must remember is that she will do whatever she feels is necessary in order to protect what she perceives to be the greater good."

We left the conference room and started walking. "I'm not defending her actions. One of the reasons I left the IGJ was over certain… policies she put in place. But Yilmaz will use you however she sees fit. You can count on one thing with her. There's always another motive behind what she says, how she acts, and even her expressions. Everything is carefully crafted to elicit the responses she's looking for," Ochoa cautioned.

"I'd gotten that impression," I replied, "but thanks for the reminder. The woman just gets under my skin."

"As she does with most. But you've outsmarted her once. Now, it's time to do it again. But"—Ochoa stopped and turned to face me—"what you did back there was both smart and stupid. Yilmaz knows two things now. She knows there's a part of you that won't play her games, and there's another part she'll be able to manipulate. If you'd been serious, a well-placed bullet in her shoulder or leg would have sealed the deal."

I blinked and stared at Ochoa. "You can't be serious."

She tilted her head to one side and stared.

I frowned and grumbled, "Yes. I get it."

"Perhaps. She believed you enough to not fully call your bluff. But next time, she won't. So if you decide to do something like that again, then you're going to have to be prepared to follow through."

I'd opened a rather nasty can of worms. And I wasn't sure I agreed with Ochoa's assessment that I'd truly outsmarted Yilmaz before. What had gone down on the *Justus* wasn't outsmarting Yilmaz but merely playing a desperate game and winning by the skin of my teeth. But Ochoa's confidence in me was nice to hear, just not the warning she was giving.

"Mahia, at one point, I had to make the same decision you're facing, when I was younger, before I signed up with the IGJ. I can't say if I regret it or not, because I've only known this kind of life, but my decision put me on the path of working in intelligence. And from there on out, I've had to know the difference between bluffing and proving a point."

I had to look away, and I wondered if she was warning me off becoming like her or merely trying to clue me in on the cost of what such decisions would be. *Pops, did you face this type of decision? Or is this just a part of who the Orions are? Merciless. Relentless in making sure we get what we want. Am I doomed to follow in my family's footsteps, or can I make my own way?*

We started walking again, and Ochoa continued. "And while Miles might appear to be many things, he's actually only one of them." We turned a corner and moved up to the next deck.

"And what's that?" I snorted.

"A little boy trying to live up to the standards placed upon him at such a young age."

"What?"

"I work for Miles for very specific reasons, one of them being what he's tried to do, how he's tried to help."

"Help? Miles? Are we talking about the same self-made madman here?"

Ochoa shook her head. "All a front."

"You're trying to flip the tables on me," I said. "Miles has proven he cares about one thing, himself. He's a master manipulator, great at tricking others into doing his bidding. Trust me, I should know."

"Yes. I won't argue he's perfected the art of manipulation, a talent he had to learn early on, growing up in the emperor's home. And I won't argue with you that he may have gone off track now and again. But Miles isn't Yilmaz. He's on your side. He'll fight for you, and dare I say, he'll die for you."

"Why are you telling me this?"

"Because you need to hear it. You need to remember you have people who believe in you and will fight with you." Ochoa stopped, and for a while, I wasn't sure what she was going to do. Then she took a deep breath and looked at me. "Working in intelligence is a lonely job. You don't make friends or allies. You have to rely upon yourself to get the job done and stay alive. I've made and destroyed friendships all for what that person could give me. And in the end, I was always alone. But since I've worked with Miles, I respect and understand the need for teams, for a network of individuals to share the burden of a job. And that's what you have. We're here to help share the burden."

Tears stung my eyes, and I looked down at my boots.

"I'm guessing you haven't heard that very often," Ochoa said quietly. "And whenever you need a reminder, all you have to do is ask."

"Thanks," I whispered.

<h1 style="text-align:center">3</h1>

Top of the Class

Ochoa's tough words of wisdom left an unsavory pit in my stomach as I considered whether I had what it took to call a bluff. *Could I have pulled the trigger? Shot Yilmaz in the leg or the shoulder?*

So I did the one thing I thought might help. I visited Miles's chef. The order would be completed by the evening, and I requested everyone come to my quarters after the crew's second rotation was finished.

In the meantime, Yilmaz came through on one part of her agreement, and scads of files were waiting for me when I returned to our hab-unit. Cain was sitting at the desk, already reading them.

I walked up behind him and slid my hands down his chest. <I really am sorry.>

He reached up and grabbed one of my hands to give it a gentle squeeze. <I know.>

"Anything good so far?" I asked.

"Mainly historical information. Once Sam finishes pulling in information from other sources, I think that will help round out the picture. But the original

Gatekeepers, the indigenous population of the Lesser Seeds, have some intriguing stories. I wouldn't consider them myths but remnants of eyewitness testimonies to events they weren't able to understand."

I moved to his side and pulled up the other chair. "How so?"

Cain closed the file he'd been reading and pulled up another one. "Here. Have a look at this: 'In the time of Lo-Liopath-Poli, Destroyer of Waktrr and Builder of the first Gate, came the darkness. The mouth of Eydrr opened, and they spat fire upon their children. And from the fire rose the vengeful tongue of Eydrr, along with the sharp teeth of Eydrr, and they feasted upon the Seed.'"

"My comparative religious studies memories are a little rusty. You're going to have to help me out here," I said.

"Eydrr is the first god of the Seeds. A combination of five distinct personalities, which are believed to be rooted in the five seasons found on the Seed of Dethron," Cain explained.

"The original home world for the Irolo, correct?" I asked.

"Point to you," Cain teased. "Xenologists and religious researchers believe this little snippet is detailing the destruction around the Seed of Karth."

"Wait, hold on." I leaned back and closed my eyes, thinking Karth sounded familiar. *Where have I recently seen it?* My eyes flew open, and I grinned. "Karth. That's where the moons were destroyed and where the Opa-li-Poli FloodGates of Knowledge were built, right?"

"Another point. Keep it up, and you might pass the course," Cain said.

I smirked. "And what will I get if I do?"

Cain blinked, and his eyes shifted from violet to amber in an instant. He didn't need to say the words—I could feel the energy radiating off him.

"One last question," he said. "Tell me what this part of the myth is describing, and you will have aced the test."

I gulped and leaned forward to read where he indicated: "'The face of Yil shone down upon her children and swallowed the darkness. And out from the belly of Yil came the Flood. And from the Flood came the Light. And from the Light came the Gate. And from the Gate came the Knowledge.'"

Waste fuel. I read through it several times. The word "Yil" was familiar, and my instincts told me it should be tagged with the information I'd remembered about Karth. We'd sat in the cafe and killed time before our meeting with the Star Eaters on Lunar 5. *But what was it referring to?*

*[Y*IL *REFERS TO THE* O*PALI* Y*IL* N*EBULA. A TOURIST CAN HAVE AN UNOBSTRUCTED VIEW OF THIS NEBULA AND WHAT THE LOCALS CONSIDER THE TOMB OF* L*O-*L*IOPATH-*P*OLI.]*

Sam? Holy rocket burners. The *Samaritan*'s AI network had remained relatively silent since we'd transferred back to the ship. She'd alerted me to a few incoming messages and requests from Lio or the others, but on the whole, our relationship had changed significantly since I handed control to Lio.

Thanks.

[The data will be finished correlating within the next seven hours. Do you wish to be alerted?]

Yes, please.

I leaned back in my chair, and a slow grin spread across my face. This would be my little secret, although I'm sure Cain sensed the little devious streak I was feeling at the moment. "Yil refers to the nebula."

He lifted an eyebrow and nodded. "Third point to you."

Thankfully, we weren't interrupted.

<We should get back to business. I invited everyone here after the second rotation,> I told Cain as I pulled the sheets over to my side of the bed.

He rolled over and grunted. *<And why did you do that?>*

<My way of apologizing.>

He sat halfway up and looked at me. "It isn't necessary. They understand the pressure you're under. We all—"

I pushed myself up and shook my head, brushing my hair out of my face. "I know. But I've…" I let my head fall back against the wall. "I want to. All those years I told myself I was perfectly fine while on my own was a stupid lie. Having you and the others, well…"

Cain reached out and brushed my cheek. "You don't have to explain."

I leaned over and kissed him. "But we really need to get back to work."

He grumbled something against my lips but eventually pulled away.

Once we were back at the desk, several alerts were waiting for us. Two more data dumps had come through, giving us more files from Yilmaz. Lio had sent an alert as well. Yilmaz had come through again, and contact had been made, so we were waiting for a reply.

Cain started sorting through the new files but stopped. "What's wrong?"

"The Eeri. I can't believe I'm actually going to be meeting with those cloud suckers. I know there are new negotiations going on and that Pops's motives are still murky, but you can't deny the damage and heartache the Eeri caused during the war. If not for Pops's involvement, I still wouldn't have any warm and fuzzy feelings for them."

"You will have to place those feelings aside," Cain said.

I glared. "That's not helpful."

"My mother would regularly meet with diplomats and governmental leaders she couldn't tolerate. Do you want to know her trick?"

"Was it a blaster tucked up her sleeve just in case?" I asked.

Cain scowled. "No. It was not. She reminded herself of the stakes at hand if she ignored everyone she disliked or preferred not to associate with."

"Wow. What a glorious revelation." Out of the corner of my eye, I caught his tail twitch.

"If we all buried our heads in the sand and worked only with those who agreed with us or saw things the way we did, what good would any of us be? How many momentous decisions have been made when two opposing forces can lay aside their differences and come together to try to make something new, something better?"

"Look, you're preaching to the choir. I get it. But it still doesn't mean I have to like it."

"I'm not saying you do. But when we meet with the Eeri—face to face—be prepared to present the side of yourself that understands what's at stake."

I stood and paced in front of the desk. "Again, I get it. Pops might have been a Sun Worshiper, but he wasn't xenophobic. He worked with and had friends from several worlds and species. I argued the same ideas with Lucas before everything went sideways. But that still doesn't diminish the fact I'm not thrilled about this, either. Everything I've thought I've known has been turned upside down, but the one constant I've had in my mind is…" *Hate?* That felt too strong. "Vehement dislike of the Eeri. And it was always the one topic I could agree with whenever anyone broached the whole subject. It gave me something in common with others."

"Perhaps that's the real issue," Cain commented.

"No. The actual issue is how can we trust them? How can we know that they're going to be telling us the truth? And we're entering into this deal because of Yilmaz. That's not the most stable of foundations, there."

Cain looked up and studied me. "You're the one who said we needed to go to the Eeri. Are you trying to tell me you're having second thoughts?"

I stopped. *Am I?* Or maybe I was just pushing back against the last piece of the puzzle, not quite ready to concede that what I knew of the Eeri could be wrong as well. I'd thought I'd been getting used to these crazy adventures my life had suddenly turned out to be.

I slumped back down in my chair. "No," I mumbled.

"Good. But I'm sure Miles can fabricate some type of inconspicuous weapon for you, if that'll help."

"Okay, who are you, and what have you done with Cain?" I asked.

He twitched his tail again but turned to face me. "You brought him back."

Heat rushed to my cheeks, and I couldn't hold his gaze. *<Me?>*

<I'd locked myself away after what happened with Elea. Committed to proving myself and to the IGJ in order to attain the ranking to open a case file for her. But now… you're reminding me of who I used to be.>

<Aren't we the pair, then?>

<Yes, I rather think we are.>

Not much work was done before everyone came over.

4

Unexpected Guests

"Is that…?" Miles asked, spying the elaborate silver tray and cover sitting on the table.

I grinned. "Sure is."

"I might have to charge a fee if everyone is going to be using his services," Miles grumbled. "Did you know Lio has also decided that my chef is now his personal chef as well?"

"Perhaps that has something to do with his being the captain," I responded.

Miles's expression darkened. "But I own this ship."

Cain joined us and handed me a steaming hot mug of krilotho, a Darquet delicacy, with spiced tea, cream, and a dash of pol, the Darquet's version of brandy.

"He never was very good at sharing his toys," Cain commented and gave Miles a blank stare over the top of his mug as he took a sip.

"And you were—" Miles was interrupted as Lio and Ochoa arrived.

When they were all comfortably seated—Miles and Cain on opposite ends of the room—I nervously cleared my throat. "Um. Well, I'm not used to this type of thing, but I wanted to apologize for my actions earlier and properly thank each one of you for sticking by me through this crazy ride." The end of my speech quickly got mashed together, and I couldn't help but blush furiously at the end. *Talk about feeling foolish.*

Miles lifted his glass and cheered, making me blush even more. And Cain didn't help at all when he stood and gave me a hug and a kiss on the cheek.

<You're more than welcome.>

"Right. Yup. So, anyway. Dig in!" I turned and lifted off the cover, revealing an elaborately decorated three-tiered cake.

Lio burst out laughing and was the first in line for a slice.

Half sugar crazed and feeling warm and fuzzy, I leaned back against Cain and listened to the banter between my friends. *My friends. Who would have thought? In a way, I guess I had Mrs. Gol to thank. If not for that crazy lady, I might not have been sitting there but back at my desk at Confore. Well, probably not.* Those pesky assassin kids might actually have accomplished their job.

But I certainly hadn't expected my life to turn out like this, especially in such a short time. And despite the concerns and anxiety I was feeling about meeting with the Eeri and figuring out how to stop the Star Eaters from destroying, well, everything, I was content.

<I don't think I've felt this way since before Epo-5, when everything went sideways. I could get used to this.>

<Good,> Cain responded.

I let my head rest on his shoulder, and my eyes drifted

shut. I would've sworn I closed them for only a few seconds before Sam interrupted.

"Code red. All crew to battle stations. Code red. All crew to battle stations," Sam's alert echoed throughout the room.

My eyes flew open, and everyone was up and dashing for the door.

"What the hell is going on?" Lio thundered as he made his way out of my quarters and charged down the hall. Ochoa and Miles were right on his heels, both already communicating with other crew members.

"Sam, what's going on?" I asked as Cain and I got to our feet.

"Proximity alert with a Jumjul destroyer-class vessel. Weapons are hot, targeting has fixated on critical systems."

Cain and I threw each other a look, and we dashed out of the room, heading for the bridge. By the time we arrived, Lio was issuing commands, and reports were filtering in.

"Have they responded?" he asked the comms station.

"No, sir. Message is broadcasting on all frequencies. Wait. Message incoming."

"Play it," Lio snapped.

"Human ship *Samaritan*, verification required."

"Where's the rest of it?" Miles asked as he walked over to the officer at comms.

"That's all of it, sir," the woman replied.

"What verification?" I asked, looking between Lio and Miles.

"My verification," Yilmaz said as Ochoa marched her onto the bridge.

Saturn's rings.

"What are you playing at?" Miles growled as he stormed up to her. "I thought we had an agreement."

"We do," she said and calmly took stock of the situation, "and I'm upholding my end of the deal. With both of you," she added, craning her neck to look at me. "You wanted to see the Eeri. Well, right now, that's only going to happen with the approval of the Jumjul. While the two may be allies concerning what's recently happened, the Jumjul will not take it well if we leave them out of the loop. You want the Eeri? Right now, that means dealing with the Jumjul first."

"You could've explained that nifty little detail earlier," Miles said.

Yilmaz shrugged. "And spoil the fun?"

"Sir, we still need the verification code," the comms officer interjected.

"Do it," Lio said. "Give them the codes. But know this—at the first sign of this going sideways, I'll make sure you never see the light of day again." His fur was standing on edge, and his lips were pulled back in a vicious snarl as he addressed Yilmaz.

"Understood, Captain," she replied.

Ochoa led her over to the comms station but made Yilmaz tell her the code, and Ochoa input it herself.

To say we all took a collective breath and held it would be a tad cliché, but we did. And we were almost blue in the face before the Jumjul replied.

"Verification code received and authenticated. Docking protocols will commence. Prepare to be boarded."

Lio marched over to the captain's chair and hit the comms button. "This is your captain. In just a few moments, we are going to be boarded by the Jumjul. All crew are to comply with Jumjul authority per article fourteen, section four, paragraphs one through twelve of the Cosway Charters. Code Teal is in effect. Repeat: Code Teal is in effect."

<*Code Teal?*> I asked Cain.

He shrugged. <*I don't know.*>

Sam? Can you tell me what Code Teal is?

[*THAT REQUIRES SECURITY CLEARANCE.*]

Really? You're going to pull that card on me now?

I didn't expect Sam to reply. The AI was supposed to function only within the parameters of her coding. But Sam answered. *Call me a scuttle crab.* And she confirmed the suspicions I'd had before. Sam had either taken a liking to me, or she was moving beyond her programming.

[*CODE TEAL IS A DIRECTIVE TO ALL CREW TO CEASE WORK ORDERS OUTSIDE ANY AGREEMENTS WITH THE JUMJUL HIGH COURTS. THE CREW MAY USE ANY MISDIRECTION NECESSARY TO PREVENT JUMJUL INTERFERENCE.*]

Wow. I wasn't expecting that. But then again, considering who owned the *Samaritan*, I really should have. And it piqued my curiosity. I wondered what Miles could've had running on the ship that he didn't want the Jumjul to know about. The possibilities were endless.

"One more thing," Yilmaz announced. "The Jumjul will expect me to be acting in accordance with my position with the InterGalactic Justice system. Not as your prisoner."

"No," Ochoa said flat out.

"Then you risk raising even more suspicion than you currently have," Yilmaz replied.

"If we don't? Then what? The Jumjul will arrest us?" I asked.

"That's the best-case scenario," Yilmaz said. "They're already on edge and tentative with any negotiations. Miles can attest to that."

The would-be emperor was furious and barely holding back his outrage. "She's correct. They've received all of our transmissions verifying Lucas Orion was killed, and the Sun Worshipers threat has been downgraded. But without confirmation of whose hands the weapon—which Lucas stole from the IGJ—has ended up in, the Jumjul aren't standing down."

"Then do it," I said, and all eyes turned toward me. *Decision time*. "This is the gamble we're going to have to take. We don't need the Jumjul on the wrong side of this. And if they're on our way to the Eeri, then that's what we do. But Yilmaz, you need to listen carefully." I stared at her. "We know your tricks. All of us. And none of us have any sympathy for you. We might be on the same side right now, from the standpoint that none of us want to see more unnecessary destruction, but if you try to play us, not one of us here will hesitate to do what's necessary."

"Understood."

I glanced at Ochoa, who gave me a small nod.

"I'm a little rusty on Jumjul protocol," I said. "Do we meet them at the airlock or wait for them here?"

"Meet them at the airlock," Miles answered. "And I suggest we all make a mad dash to our closets and change into formal uniforms. They're sticklers for such things."

"I'll see to Yilmaz," Ochoa said.

"Good. The rest of you, we'll meet at…" Lio glanced over at the security station.

"Deck Three, transfer hub four, sir."

5

A Private Message

Besides my Confore Tech uniform, I'd never had to wear anything more than a cozy jumpsuit. I hated formal dress. The high collar was silently attacking me, and I itched all over. Lio had two uniforms fabricated for Cain and me, and while he looked right at home in the smart outfit, I didn't.

<Stop fussing.>

<Don't even start with me. I'm not in the mood.> I reached up and tried to tug on my collar, but the material was strictly no-stretch.

"Attention," Lio called out as he walked down the row of officers in the transfer hub. "Eyes down. No direct eye contact is to be made unless they give you permission to speak. Then remember it is only a glance up then eyes back down, to show respect. Clear?"

"Yes, sir," everyone called out.

"If you do not know the answer to a question, you will make your apologies and excuse yourself. Then the next highest ranking officer will respond. Clear?"

"Yes, sir."

<*I feel like I'm in a recruitment vid or something.*>
<*Don't remind me.*>

I shot Cain an incredulous look. <*You were in an* IGJ *recruitment vid? Jupiter. That, I've got to see.*>

<*No. You don't.*>

"All answers are to be kept short and succinct. Stay within the bounds of the question asked. Do not open any discussions into areas the Jumjul aren't asking about. Clear?"

"Yes, sir!"

Sam's voice rang out. "Docking cycle complete. Prepare to be boarded."

<*Have you ever met a Jumjul?*> I asked.

<*No. My mother met with a representative of the High Court twice. But both times, she refused to allow me to join her, even at the dinner functions.*>

That little nugget of information didn't boost my confidence at all. I'd seen them on vids and newscasts but never in real life. If one species existed, besides the Eeri, that I wouldn't mind never having direct contact with, it was the Jumjul. Plainly put, they scared the hell out of me—a no-nonsense species whose religion centered on mathematics and various branches of study related to numbers. Math had never been my strong suit. But putting a toe out of line with the Jumjul could result in being sent off to a penal colony world before anyone could say "Pluto." *How Yilmaz expects me, of all people, to navigate the Jumjul in order to reach the Eeri…* Well, the odds weren't great. *Maybe that's what she's counting on.*

The transfer hub door hissed and slid open. And despite Lio's warning, I couldn't help but sneak a glance.

Seeing a Jumjul in person was terrifying yet oddly enchanting. I felt the strangest urge to start up a plushie company—cute, cuddly little Jumjul that, when you squeeze them, turn into face-eating monsters. I doubted a gigantic market existed for something like that.

<Stop staring,> Cain said. *<And don't you dare even think about it. They have three venomous glands, two of which are in their palms, and a third that mixes with their saliva.>*

<I wasn't really going to try to hug one. Sheesh.>

Jumjuls were no taller than the average human and were covered in fur. But they weren't a homogenous color. Each Jumjul was different, sometimes only a shade darker or lighter than a neighbor whose fur was in the same color family. I'd always wondered if the colors indicated a cultural system or if they were pure random biological chance.

Their eyes were enormous and compound, reminding me of several invertebrate insects from Old Earth. Their biology seemed a strange mixture of mammalian and insectoid. Despite the unusual combination, the large eyes and soft fur gave them a deceptively sweet and innocent look. But behind that innocence were incredible minds and the fierceness of warriors. Their military prowess was unmatched. Their exterior appearance was the perfect trap—lure in the unsuspecting prey with their cuteness, and then, *bam!* It was chow time.

"Commandant Yilmaz," a Jumjul said as it stepped onto the *Samaritan.*

"Here." Yilmaz stepped out from Ochoa's side and faced the Jumjul. "On behalf of the InterGalactic Justice system, we thank you for your aid."

"You will forfeit your stocks on penalty of perjury."

"Of course," Yilmaz replied and stepped back into line.

"Coordinates have been sanctified and approved. The Majmul give their blessings. You are fortunate."

A second, then a third Jumjul joined the first. The Jumjul who had boarded were all in the same blue color family, just varying shades. Of course, the different weapons slung across their torsos were a helpful way to identify them too.

"The captain of the *Samaritan* will escort us to the bridge."

Lio stepped out of the line. "This way." He turned to face his crew. "Fall out."

I started to move, but Cain grabbed my arm. <*Wait. We must leave in groups of seven.*>

<*Geez. Thanks.*>

That literally could have been a big misstep. And I shouldn't have been surprised when the crew Lio had requested to be present could split off into three groups of seven each.

Cain and I were a part of the last group, and when the coast was clear, I let out a huge sigh of relief. "Now what?" I asked. "To the bridge?"

"No. We'll wait until we're called for. If we even are," Cain said. "Come on."

I didn't care for being left out of what was happening, but I wasn't prepared to go toe-to-toe with the Jumjul. *Sam, if anything important happens, can you fill me in?*

[*Affirmative.*]

Yeah, she definitely had a soft spot for me.

When we got back to our hab-unit, I started to change, but Cain stopped me.

"Better to be ready, just in case," he said.

"You've got to be kidding me. I will not stay in this death trap. If they need us, then I'll change back. But while we're in our quarters, I'm going to be comfortable."

Displeased, Cain swished his tail back and forth, but he chose not to argue. *Wise man.*

Comfortably tucked away in my jumpsuit, I settled in behind the desk and pulled up Yilmaz's files. Many were left to read through, and Sam hadn't finished correlating the databases yet.

Just when I got through a rather long-winded explanation of the leading theory of the functioning of the tech that held the FloodGates of Knowledge, Sam interrupted.

[THE JUMJUL HAVE REQUESTED THE IMMEDIATE SURRENDER OF THE SAMARTIAN. LIO HAS ISSUED A COMMAND THAT ALL CREW MEMBERS COMPLY.]

"What?" I sat up.

Cain, sensing my immediate change in mood, tensed.

"Sam? Can you repeat that?"

[THE JUMJUL HAVE REQUESTED—INCOMING MESSAGE. PRIVATE CHANNEL. PLAY MESSAGE?]

"Yes, of course!"

"Mahia, what's going—"

"Hush."

["IF YOU WANT TO SEE THIS THROUGH, HEAD TO DECK ELEVEN, SHUTTLE BAY FIVE. BE READY TO FIGHT."]

"Sam, who sent the message?"

She didn't respond. *Pluto's dilemma.* I filled Cain in on

what Sam said, and he tried to get a hold of Miles, but he wasn't answering. We poked our heads out of the room and snagged the first person running past. She confirmed Sam's message.

Not taking time to debate where the private message had come from, we grabbed what we could and high-tailed it out of there. No way was the message from the Jumjul, and if it was one of Yilmaz's traps, we would deal with it when we arrived. But right then, we had to rely on trust.

The crew was foaming at the mouth, so to speak. Everyone was running through the corridors, shouting orders or looking panicked. This was the worst-case scenario with the Jumjul. If they were seizing the ship, they would consider everyone within guilty. Resistance meant death.

Cain tried again to connect with Miles then Lio and, lastly, Ochoa. But none of them responded. We raced to Deck Eleven and skidded to a halt as Cain flung out an arm and pushed me down a darkened corridor. He wrapped his arms around me and clamped a hand over my mouth.

<*What is it?*> I asked, unable to keep the terror out of my head.

Cain had never responded to a situation that way before.

<*Keep quiet. And still. When I tell you, move with me.*>

I didn't argue.

I tried to calm my breathing and match the rise and fall of my chest to his. But not only was I on high alert—Cain was too. And though he usually kept a strong check on his emotions, they were spilling over and mixing with mine.

<On the count of three, we're going to move to the left. There's a door ten paces from us. We'll hold just next to it. Then move into the room on my mark. One… two… three. Move.>

Without our heart's blood connection, our coordination attempt would've been a hilarious failure. But we moved in sync. We stopped where he indicated, and after a few seconds, we slipped into the room, a commissary. *Well, this brings back memories.*

Cain moved us to the farthest corner and tucked us down behind a few chairs. *<If they're using heat sensors or hacking into the HalfLife systems, we won't have long until they find us.>*

<How did you know?>

<Training. They're sweeping this deck. If that door opens, we have two options. Surrender… or fight.>

He didn't have to ask the implicit question. Someone had warned us and was waiting for us. But even if that wasn't true, only one answer remained. I would not give up, not then, not after everything we'd been through.

Cain understood. *<Get behind me.>*

The fools that we were, I wasn't armed. I hadn't felt the need. But thankfully, the years of being with the IGJ had given Cain the habit of always carrying a weapon. As quietly as I could, I moved behind him, ducking behind his back as he got into a defensive posture. And I sorely wished I had a weapon of my own.

<They're five paces out from the door.>

<How do you know that?>

<Intuition and telepathy, remember?>

<*Right.*> I paused then added, <*Cain, I*—>

<*I know.*> A rush of warmth and love washed over me. I let myself cherish the feelings for a moment, then I pushed them down and tried to settle my mind and nerves.

<*At the door.*>

We heard the sound of weapons fire in the hallway, but it was over as quickly as it began.

The door opened, and Cain tensed, ready to defend us.

"Come on. We've only got a few minutes before they send backup. Well? What are you waiting for?" Yilmaz snapped.

6

Sacrifices Made

Cain dragged my incredulous self out into the corridor, and I about fainted as Yilmaz helped a wounded Miles to his feet.

"Come on," she hissed. "If I can track you, then you know they will too."

We didn't have far to go before we reached the shuttle bay.

"Here," Yilmaz said. "Take him."

I slung Miles's arm over my shoulder and cringed at the amount of blood staining the front of his uniform.

"Cain, on my mark."

"Yes, sir." Cain moved to the other side of the door without considering who had given the order.

Yilmaz counted down, and together, she and Cain barged into the shuttle bay. When the coast was clear, I quickly followed suit, half dragging Miles with me.

"It's the far one. On the left," he whispered.

I relayed the information, and Cain took Miles's other arm while Yilmaz raced to the shuttle and prepped for launch.

"What happened?" I asked as we got Miles up into the shuttle and laid him out on a bench. "How bad is it? Where are the medical supplies?"

He raised an arm and pointed at a locker above him. Cain reached over, grabbed the med kit, and began triage as best he could.

"We've got incoming," Yilmaz said. "Heads up." She stalked past us, toward the side of the hatch. "Looks like one life sign, and it's… Damn." She punched the control, and the hatch door slid open. "Get in. Quick."

I looked up, expecting Ochoa or Lio, but was surprised to see the Master Glipglow. As the door sealed shut again, Yilmaz whipped around and pressed the muzzle of her gun into the master's back. "How did you know where to go?"

The master's lower jaw opened and closed several times before he answered. "Biosigns. We have a trace program running to monitor Mahia Orion's biosigns. In case the need arose for further data."

I should've felt a little outraged, but honestly, I was glad. The master had been tucked away in his lab, and I'm ashamed to admit I'd forgotten about him in all the hubbub.

"Can you help him?" I asked and pointed at Miles.

"Yes." The master got to work while Yilmaz kept her weapon trained on him.

"Put it down," I snapped. "He's on our side. What the hell happened?"

"The Star Eaters. Exactly like I said they would," Yilmaz snapped. She holstered her weapon and headed for the cockpit. "This old bird better have the firepower you promised."

"You better believe it," Miles muttered.

Cain and I took one look at each other and followed Yilmaz. I knew the master would take care of Miles. I had to have faith in something.

"You better cough up a better explanation," I said. "How do we know this isn't some elaborate ruse? To separate us?"

Yilmaz didn't look up from the controls as she answered. "If that was the case, do you think I'd leave you with those who make you strong? I'd have dumped Miles, and I wouldn't allow your heart's blood to be joining us either."

Her explanation made sense. But a carefully prepared one would.

"Cain, go talk to Miles."

<And tell me what he says, while I talk to Yilmaz. We'll compare notes.>

Cain vanished back down into the small passenger-and-cargo hold of the shuttle.

"Right. Details," I demanded as I sat down in the copilot's chair.

"The Star Eaters have been sighted in the Erith system. Word is they've totally decimated Igridian Prime. Reports are coming in that the sun's core has begun to shrink and is ejecting gas and dust."

I wasn't up to date on the latest in the astronomy schools. Truthfully, I wasn't even up to date on the old stuff, but I knew enough to know what she was saying was bad—really bad—and impossible.

"If your brother hadn't stolen the weapon—and gods know who has it now—then the IGJ would have targeted Igridian Prime and done what they needed to do in order to stop the Star Eaters," Yilmaz said. "The shuttle's prepped and ready. This is our one shot to get out of here." She turned to stare at me. "It's now or never."

This was a deal with the proverbial devil.

<Do it.> Cain's voice resonated loud and clear in my thoughts. *<Miles is confirming everything plus more.>*

"Go," I said. "What do I need to do?"

"Can you fly?"

"Not really. I've gotten the basics."

"Good enough," Yilmaz said. "Switching stations. You've got nav, and I'm taking over the weapons. I've already input the coordinates. Just keep us along that flight path, but dodge whatever you have to. Clear?"

"Sure." I scanned the controls and felt reasonably comfortable. *That we're all going to die.* "You're taking us to the Eeri?"

"Yes. It's our only chance now. The Jumjul believe it's all been a trick. A ruse. I can't say I blame them. They're rightly paranoid after what happened with Lucas. And it doesn't help that the damned emperor has tried to take the initiative for once. But the Eeri will want confirmation of what's happening. Even though they've publicly backed the Jumjul, they'll be cautious, which gives us a narrow window of time to get to them."

"The cargo bay doors are cycling open. Prepare for takeoff in three... two... one..."

<Hold on.>

The shuttle rose and followed the autopilot procedures for departure. Once we were clear of the *Samaritan*, I was fairly sure we wouldn't make it out alive. Two Jumjul destroyer-class ships loomed over the *Samaritan*, making it look like a child's toy.

"Bring us to port with a seventy-three-degree rotation," Yilmaz instructed. "Keep us on the flight path. Steady."

I keyed in the commands and waited.

"Port, not starboard," she snapped.

Whoops. I quickly fixed my mistake and waited with bated breath.

"We are being targeted. Prepare to take a direct hit. Shields at maximum."

A pair of hands gripped my shoulders.

<I didn't see this coming.>

He squeezed my shoulders in response. *<Together, remember?>*

The blast rocked our shuttle, and alerts flew up all over the place.

"Shields down to thirty-three percent," I reported. "Leaking—"

"Preparing to return fire!" Yilmaz shouted over me. "And firing!"

Whatever illicit weapons Miles had outfitted this shuttle with were powerful enough to knock out a gun turret on the Jumjul ship.

"How long until the overdrive engine is hot?" Yilmaz asked.

As I scanned my screen, trying to find the readout for the engines, Cain leaned over my shoulder and pointed. "One minute and three seconds," he replied for me.

"Hold—" Yilmaz started.

We took another round of fire. Cain was knocked to one side, but he assured me he was fine and regained his footing. He turned toward the small screen embedded above me to my right, to assess the damage.

"Rerouting power to the—" he began.

"Incoming!" Yilmaz said.

"Shields down to fourteen percent. Another hit, and we're done," Cain said. "I'm pushing everything I can to the shields without compromising the engines. Forty-two seconds to go."

"Returning fire," Yilmaz said and took out two more gun turrets. But our little shuttle wasn't a match for the Jumjul, not to mention the fact that only one of their ships was firing so far.

[Linking nav system with shuttle Elea.]

If I hadn't been mentally preparing myself for the inevitable, I would've realized two things. Sam was up to something, and Miles had named this shuttle after Cain's sister.

[Emergency evacuation orders have been issued. Pods aligned with shuttle's flight path. It's been an honor, Mahia Orion.]

Wait, what? Then my brain caught up. *Sam, no!*

"The second Jumjul ship is powering up weapons," Yilmaz reported.

"Thirty-one seconds until overdrive engines are hot," Cain said.

"Wait, Sam! Hook me up with the *Samaritan* now!" I shouted, blindly looking at the controls.

"No time," Yilmaz snapped just as Cain responded with "The ship's gone dark."

"Firing with autolock targets. Prepare to take return—"

"Twelve seconds," Cain said. "Flip controls over to the overdrive engines."

I scrambled to keep up and do as they were telling me. "Overdrive engaged."

"Ten…"

"Incoming. Brace yourself—"

But the return fire never hit us. The *Samaritan* exploded, taking a solid chunk of both Jumjul ships with her. As we stared in disbelief at the destruction raining down around us, the shuttle's overdrive engines roared to life, and we disappeared into Eeri-controlled space.

7

Light and Life

The shuttle was silent for several hours, aside from the occasional update from Yilmaz, who'd taken over nav. None of us could do anything. While the *Samaritan*'s sacrifice had allowed us to escape, we had enough data to know that it hadn't completely crippled the Jumjul vessels. The scans didn't show they were pursuing us, and neither did they pick up any other objects coming along with us. But that wasn't completely unexpected. The *Samaritan*'s escape pods would've been incredibly tiny, likely too small to be picked up on our scans. And they weren't equipped with overdrive engines. If the Jumjul took mercy upon the crew, they would scoop up the pods and imprison the survivors. If they weren't—well, I couldn't bear to think about that.

I'd pulled my legs up onto my seat and wrapped my arms around them, curled into a tight ball. Cain had taken the seat behind me, and the master continued to monitor Miles.

Sam had been a friend, perhaps. I wasn't sure I would've used that word to describe my relationship with the AI before, but Sam had been just as much a part of the crew as the rest of us, and she'd helped me escape a lot of bad. If not for her, we would've still been stuck on the *Justus* or worse.

I should've paid more attention to my gut feelings that Sam had gone outside her programming and showed a unique fondness for me. Why, though, I didn't have a clue. I was one of several who had been linked to her over time. *What made me so unique? Or so horrible? If not for me, the* Samaritan *might've made it out of the scuffle.*

<The ship might have, but not the AI system,> Cain added quietly. *<The Jumjul do not tolerate AI sentience.>*

I'd forgotten. The Jumjul and the Glipglow were both against AI technology, especially regarding possible sentience. And I was confident that's what Sam had become, intentionally or not.

The master's voice interrupted the silence. "The patient would like to speak with you."

I needed a few seconds to settle my thoughts, wipe away tears, and move back to where he'd secured Miles.

I carefully sat down on the edge of the bench and took stock of the would-be emperor. He was pale but not death's-door pale. And someone had changed him out of his bloodstained uniform into a plain jumpsuit. His eyes flickered open when I reached out and gently took his hand.

Just as sure as I was about Sam's sentience, I was also confident that Miles had either orchestrated her ability to exceed her programming, or at least turned a blind eye to what was going on with his ship.

"I'm sorry," I whispered.

He squeezed my hand in return. "The *Samaritan* was my favorite out of those four sister ships. And the one I spent most of my credits outfitting." He closed his eyes and heaved a long sigh. "All of those lives. Lost. My senior officers were on board. Several had been with me since my escape from my brother's prison, not to mention the ship herself."

"Sam sent me a message," I said, prompting Miles to open his eyes again. "She told me she'd issued emergency evacuation orders and tagged the pods with our flight trajectory."

"A noble sentiment. But the pods aren't—"

"Outfitted with overdrive engines, yes, I know," I finished for him. "But perhaps they moved far enough out to not get caught in the debris radius."

"Perhaps."

We let the rest of the unspoken reality hang between us.

"What happened?" I asked.

Even though I'd asked Cain to corroborate Yilmaz's intel with Miles, the insane situation hadn't allowed us to fully compare notes.

"The Jumjul received an update over a concerning disruption in the… Erith system? One of the planets had been invaded, and its inhabitants reported some type of biochemical weapon literally eating through the entire population."

I blinked back another round of tears and looked away. I knew exactly what the biochemical weapon had to be. *But that doesn't make sense. The Third has changed. Been able to reclaim its original purpose since it rejoined with the two*

Star Eaters. Or… I shuddered at the thought. *What if the Third hasn't really changed, though? What if everything I've gone through had no lasting effects? Could their alterations even be reversed, returned to what they originally were?*

"There were also reports of disturbances to the system's sun. The Clarion Research Team had a field station in the system," Miles said.

"That name sounds familiar," I murmured.

"It should. The Clarion Research Team is a joint effort between multiple worlds, a darling of a news story for the media right now."

"Something about studying the composition of various suns, right?"

Miles nodded. "You got it. In a way, we're lucky they were there, or else I doubt we would've fully known what was going on."

"Wait, you're sure the reports talked about problems with the sun and something on the planet?" I asked.

Miles nodded. "Yes, and the Jumjul reacted as poorly as you might have guessed. They were barely on the fence of believing us about stopping Lucas, then these reports came flooding in. Their first reaction was to lock down the ship. But I had a few plans in place for something of that nature. Lio and Ochoa were able to lock them out of the bridge, and Yilmaz… well, if not for that damned woman, I would be dead."

"So at least she's telling us the truth," I said. But my mind was caught on the fact that both things were happening together. If I'd truly helped the Third, they wouldn't need to feed off any biological life. *So why were they harvesting light and life?*

"As far as I can tell," Miles added. "She was as much caught off guard as the rest of us. Just good timing that we'd eased up on her restraints."

When Miles coughed a few times, the master stood and checked his biosigns. "He needs rest."

"Alright." I leaned down and placed a kiss on Miles's cheek, not ready to share my concerns—not even with Cain.

He gave me a grin and a wink.

"You'd better heal and fast."

"Never fear, my dear." He turned his head and closed his eyes.

I let Miles rest and turned to the master. "How are you faring?"

He opened and closed his lower jaw. "Adequate. We are satisfied that our hatchlings will continue even if we do not."

"I'm sorry you got dragged into this mess," I said.

"We are not. You present a fascinating case to study, and we are grateful for the data we've accumulated."

"Speaking of—any more ideas yet?" I asked.

The Glipglow clicked one nail against the edge of the bunk opposite Miles. "Not as yet. But we are continuing to monitor."

I gave him a nod, moved back up to the copilot's chair, and swiveled around to face Cain, who was staring at the back of Yilmaz's head.

"Can you tell him to stop?" she asked.

"No," I replied. "Where exactly are we headed?"

"To the Eeri."

"Yilmaz," I said in warning.

"Before the Jumjul incident, your captain was tracking an Eeri scout ship. I'd say they were already curious about what was happening. Right now, they're going to be our best bet. We're roughly four hours out from making contact."

"And what if they take a disliking to us?"

"A little late for that line of thinking. But something tells me they're not going to," Yilmaz confidently replied.

"Explain," Cain interjected.

"We have information they're going to want."

<She's not going to be helpful,> I commented to Cain. *<Just leave it for now. I don't think we've got too many options. If the Star Eaters are truly beginning… whatever it is that they're going to do, then we need to talk with the Eeri. And if they don't have the answers we need, well, I think we've run out of options.>*

<We should alert my mother.>

That was something I wouldn't have thought of in a million years. While Cain had never explicitly come out and said it, I knew his relationship with his mother was strained.

"Do it," I said.

Cain and I switched places, but as he placed his fingers on the controls, Yilmaz reached out and grabbed his hands.

"What do you think you're doing?" she demanded.

The somber atmosphere of mourning vanished with that reckless gesture. Cain growled, flying out of his chair and wrestling Yilmaz to the ground.

"Never touch me again," he said through clenched teeth, his canines bared. He had her down before I could even try to react.

"Careful," I said, the word of caution really meant for both of them. *<Until we can deal with the Eeri on our own, we still need her.>*

<We don't. We can find them on our own.>

"I apologize," Yilmaz said, shocking us both. "Forgive the intrusion. I was merely concerned about what you might inadvertently do. Not only will the Jumjul be working on tracing our flight path, but anything that appears suspicious right now will only put the Eeri further on edge."

<She's definitely playing nice. She wants something. Or needs something. I want this to play out.>

Cain didn't agree, given the way he snapped his tail back and forth.

<Cain. Let her up.>

With a low growl, he slowly got up, and Yilmaz raised her hands in defeat as she climbed back into the pilot's chair.

"We are going to alert the chancellor. If we die or are captured, then someone needs to know the truth of what has happened," Cain stated.

Yilmaz appeared to consider his reasoning then nodded. "Let me read it before you send it."

I felt the struggle within Cain, but he eventually nodded. "Fine."

As Cain composed the message, I slipped back to the rear of the shuttle to talk over a few worst-case scenario plans with the master. They understood and agreed that if the time should come, they would help with Yilmaz. Ochoa had talked about having to decide when the time came. Well, the time had come. And I'd made my decision.

8

Nefarious Talons

Chancellor Heron. Urgent message. Your eyes only. From Turen ed-Suren.

The Star Eaters have become a viable threat to the known worlds. They are to be considered extremely dangerous. The Erith system has been compromised and should be quarantined. You're instructed to contact Subcommandant Hild of the IGJ as soon as possible and request the Gatekeeper records from Commandant Yilmaz's private server. The access code is alpha tango seven nine one delta beta one six five alpha one tango. The subcommandant will need to provide the backup biometric scan in order to complete the security codes. Tell the subcommandant you have sunburnt access.

Be careful.

I read through the message several times. "You're sure? What if someone else hacks the encryptions?"

Yilmaz shrugged. "If they do, then they'll get access to the files and know what's going on. Even if the whisper nets pick it up and word spreads, it would still be better than silence. If we fail, someone needs to know."

As Cain encrypted the message and hit send, I leaned back in the chair as the full weight of what I'd been a part of finally hit me. I'd answered a call for help, but I'd set something horrible loose within the known worlds.

"You'd better be right about the Eeri," I said.

"You're about to find out. The scout ship must've picked us up on their radar faster than I'd calculated. They're roughly half an hour out."

I sat up a little taller, and my chest tightened. In half an hour, I would come face-to-face with those cloud suckers.

"How is Miles?" Yilmaz asked.

"Resting," I replied. "Why?"

"We'll need everyone on their feet." She turned to face me. "I was truthful when I said I've dealt with the Eeri before. But never face to face. They're reclusive, even on the best of terms. We need to be mobile and have options."

"I'll talk with the master," Cain said and left.

"What makes you think we'll get lucky a second time if there's a fight? We're outmanned and outgunned by unimaginable odds. We're walking to our doom or worse."

Yilmaz leaned back and raised an eyebrow. "Our doom? That's dramatic."

"I think the situation calls for it."

"Orions," she muttered.

"What's that supposed to mean?" I asked.

"I spent a fair amount of time chatting with your father because of his unfortunate choice of actions during the war," she remarked casually. "I was able to get a good feel for how the Orion family operates."

"You're pretty casual with your words, considering you're crammed in a shuttle with a group of people who vehemently dislike you," I snarled. *She's toying with me. Calm it down.* I took a deep breath and tried to school my face into a neutral expression, but I'd never quite mastered that like Pops or Lucas. "I think you're going to be sorely disappointed if you think you know how I'm going to play this."

For the first time in quite a while, Yilmaz actually grinned. "Good."

Enough of this. I didn't care whether I could play it as cool as Europa in the summer, I was out of there.

"How's he doing?" I asked Cain as I joined him and the master watching over Miles trying to stand and take a few steps.

"He's going to be fine," Miles said through gritted teeth. "Nothing my bioupgrades and the good doc here can't take care of."

"With all the credits you have at your disposal, I would've expected you to do a few flip stands by now," Cain commented.

Miles turned to stare at him with an open mouth.

"It's the new him," I said with a smirk. "You've got a run for your credits now."

"Huh," Miles grunted.

Watching him sway back and forth and have to sit back down was concerning.

"Seriously, though. I would've thought your bioupgrades would've taken care of the worst of the damage by now," I said.

"The Jumjul maintain an impressive array of stunner weaponry, capable of severely disabling the best bioupgrades. They equip their stunners with a nanotechnology encoded with a seek-and-destroy prerogative—an impressive level of sophistication many have expressed a desire to study. But the Jumjul continue to evade our attempts to collaborate," the master explained.

"Peachy," Miles said as he tried to stand again.

"He should be at fifty percent operational capacity within the hour," the master added, "provided he does not sustain further damage."

"Is there anything else you can do for him?" I asked.

"The supplies on this shuttle are subpar."

"Hey," Miles protested, "I've kept this shuttle up to date and stocked with the latest gadgets."

I would've sworn the Glipglow sniffed in disdain. "For a human, but certainly not for the standards we are accustomed to working with."

I stepped between the two of them. "Thank you for all that you've done. It's greatly appreciated. Isn't it, Miles?"

When he took a second too long to answer, I was tempted to step on his foot but was gracious enough not to. Finally, he ground out a very poor apology. But the master merely bowed and settled back down on the bench.

"If you're finished?" Yilmaz interrupted. She was leaning against the framework separating the two areas of the shuttle. "I dread belaboring a point, but we need options."

"We introduce ourselves and ask for a nice little sit-down chat," Miles muttered as he reached out to support himself.

"And you need options because you're really flying dark here, aren't you?" I interjected. "That's what you've been hinting at. You've dealt with them, but not like this. Before, it was from a position of power, and you probably had others working with you and intermediaries. And you've said you've never met with them face-to-face. And you're supposed to be the expert here."

"They're not to be trifled with, and they can't abide lies," Yilmaz said.

"And they've worked with you before?" Miles half joked.

Yilmaz continued, ignoring Miles. "They don't like trading or sharing information. The concessions that were given in order to bring them to the table before the war were substantial. There's very little known about their culture, religious outlook, or societal organization. But we know they're formidable, and we don't want to upset them again."

"And they know about the Star Eaters," I said. "Basically, we're walking in blind. Except we're going to be using your name to gain a foot in the door. Then we tell them—everything."

"And a backup plan?" she asked.

<I'm not sure there is one at this point,> Cain commented silently.

I agreed.

"We'll just have to wing it," I told her, "which might not be how you're used to working, but so far, the universe has seen fit to keep me alive through some of the dumbest ideas I've had. Let's see if my luck continues to hold."

She was *not* happy at all. But I didn't care. She spun around and headed back to the pilot's seat. Miles let out a long sigh.

"Is it really that bad?" Cain asked.

"Let's just say I'm glad we've buried the hatchet. Or else you might've been able to tick me off your list," Miles said.

I sat down next to Miles and kept my voice low. "We really should have a backup plan, but I agree with Cain that there really isn't one at this point. What do you think?"

"We've already provided one," the master said, causing us all to turn and stare.

"Come again?" I asked.

"Due to the nature of our situation, we will share something rarely told to those outside of the dens." The master raised the upper hand on his left side. "The claw of the middle finger on this hand is equipped with a locator beacon, to be activated for emergencies only. We felt confident this was an emergency."

I gaped at the Glipglow. "Are you telling me an army of Glipglows is going to be headed this way?"

"A few ships will be sent to investigate. In the advent of our death or severe injury, the beacon will adjust accordingly, as will the dens."

I'd been in awe of Glipglow talons, but this took my appreciation to a whole new level. The power it had to be laced with in order to send such a signal—I couldn't wrap my mind around it.

"And you didn't see fit to bring this up with Yilmaz?" Miles asked.

The master looked at me. "We thought the commandant was not included in this den."

Miles scooted to the edge of the bench and bowed his head. "It is my great honor to be included in your den, and I humbly submit myself as a hatchling in your presence. My life is your life."

I could feel the vibration of the master's rumble and took it as a sign of acceptance and gratitude. I leaned forward as did Cain. "We also are honored to be included in your den and submit ourselves as your hatchlings. Our lives are your lives." The rumble continued as we straightened. *<I'm not entirely sure what we've just committed to,>* I confessed to Cain.

<While there may be commitments down the road—if we survive this—this honor is rarely given. And you did right by following Miles's lead.>

I did feel a pang of guilt at remembering how I'd forgotten to invite the master to the impromptu get-together with the cake before the Jumjul arrived, but I also allowed myself a tiny moment of good cheer, knowing I had indeed made another friend.

The moment didn't last long.

"Heads up. We've got company!" Yilmaz shouted.

We all stood, but I stopped Miles. "No. Stay here. Get every bit of rest that you can. It won't do us any good if you overdo it right now."

He frowned but nodded.

Cain and I took up our positions beside Yilmaz and looked at the shuttle's readouts.

"Two scout ships approaching, but weapons aren't reading hot," Cain said.

"Any messages?" I asked.

"No. There are no signals being broadcast at all. I'm sending out the universal distress call, encoded with my confirmation bio ID."

"Keep sending it. Hopefully, they'll—"

And just like that, we got confirmation that the Eeri had indeed perfected zap 'n' roll technology.

Errors

<Cain?>

Everything was pitch black, and I was sitting on something cold and hard. A floor was my best guess.

<I'm here. Do you know where you are? I can sense you. I don't think you're far.>

<It's completely dark. I can't make anything out. What about the others?>

<They're with me. We're in some kind of holding cell. Comfortable, at least, and have been provided food and water. But so far, we can't find a way to get out. Yilmaz says she doesn't know what's going on. But I don't believe her.>

So much for the gamble of making a deal with the devil and having it turn out to be useless. If she's even telling the truth. *<Are any of you hurt? Have you made contact yet?>*

<No. You?>

<Nope. Wait, hold on. I think I hear something.> Something clicked faintly in front of me, and a bank of lights gradually came to life. As my eyes adjusted, I looked around. My guess had been correct. I was sitting on the floor of what I assumed was my delightful new

cell. *What a lovely little glass box.* I stood and stretched, my fingertips brushing the ceiling. When I spread my arms out to the sides, I had a bit more room, at least. *<We're going to have to find another realtor. This cramped living area isn't cutting it for me.>*

<Focus on your breathing and not the size of the space.>

<Easy for you to say, Mr. We Got Food and Water. Let's switch places, please?>

<If I could...>

A shadow passed overhead, and without thinking, I ducked. When I cautiously stood to take a look, nothing appeared to be there.

"Hello?" I called out, knowing that was a straight up horror-vid move. "Anyone there? You should know we come in peace." *Good grief. Stop being so cliché.* "Look, I don't know what your cultural customs are or what protocols you consider polite, but we came here for your help. It has to do with the Star Eaters."

The lights went out, and I heard skittering noises above me and below. *Shit.*

<Mahia!> Adrenaline and panic surged through our connection, and I got the vague sense he was pounding against something, desperate to break free. Plus, he was really annoyed at his newfound roommates yelling questions and advice at him.

Something somewhere inside my room hissed with displeasure, and I backed up until I pressed up against the wall. The whispers increased, and I bit my lip to keep from crying out. *Breathe, just like Cain said. Breathe. You've come here for a reason.*

I reminded myself of the old adage "Fake it until you

make it." I stepped away from the wall, took another deep breath, and closed my eyes. *<I'm alright. There's no need for your shouting. You're going to give me a headache.>* That did not soothe Cain.

I opened my eyes and looked up at the ceiling. "My name is Mahia Orion. You've worked with my pops before, Wats Hawking Orion. We've come here because we need your help. Commandant Yilmaz told me that you could help us with the Star Eaters."

The lights flared to life again, and some instructions followed.

"The stars are to be cultivated. The Errors will be reclaimed. Stay within your nexus, and the Purified will decide the reaping."

The instructions were as clear as waste fuel, except for that first line. I had a bad feeling about what that was alluding to. The sound of something scurrying above and below me resumed, along with the stupid whispers. To say I was scared out of my gourd would've been the understatement of the entire misadventure, starting with redeeming my vacation voucher. If we survived and I ever wanted to lease my rights to some vid company, I was sure I would make a killing. But I forced myself to keep calm. *You've been in unpleasant situations before. This is a piece of cake.*

"We need your help. The Star Eaters have begun to destroy a solar system, and we've got to stop them. Can you help us with that?"

The lights grew brighter and focused on a spot in the middle of my cube. I also realized the walls were turning transparent. I stepped to one side to try to see what was beyond my little home away from home. Similar cuboid structures appeared to be suspended all around me. *In… air? A vacuum?*

The idea of a decontamination zone made sense, except for the fact that they'd separated me from the others. Well, that wasn't really true. I sighed. Their singling me out *did* make sense. I was an Orion, after all. But I was sure of one thing—the space I was seeing didn't seem small enough to fit inside one of their scout-class ships.

<Cain? Does it look like you're in a plastic cube? Can you see out beyond it?>

I waited for his answer, and when he did, he confirmed my suspicions.

"The Error must inhabit the center of the orbiter."

"I don't understand what that means," I said.

"The Error must inhabit the center of the orbiter."

I stepped back from the wall and slowly turned in a circle, trying to detect any kind of glitch that might indicate some kind of surveillance system. *Nothing. Nada.*

"The Error must inhabit the center of the orbiter."

I was feeling a bit more frustrated than scared. We hadn't come with any intention to disobey their cultural customs, but without some kind of frame of reference, I was at a loss for how to comply.

"You're going to have to help me out. I don't know what those terms are referencing. What is the Error?"

After a renewed wave of whispers, a different voice said, "You are the Error."

"Okay. That's helpful… but harsh." But if I was the Error, then I assumed I needed to stand in the center of my little cube or, rather, the orbiter. So I complied, fervently hoping that would signal I wasn't a threat. Generating a bit of goodwill was the main goal.

"The Error will remain still during deconstruction."

"Deconstruction?" *Whoops. Dumb, dumb, dumb.*

I tried to take a step back but couldn't. Another bright light had sprung to life, engulfing and paralyzing me, except for my mouth.

"Please tell me you're not taking the word *deconstruction* literally. I'm not really prepared to be taken apart piece by piece yet."

"The Error will remain still during deconstruction."

A shimmering screen appeared in front of me, and a wealth of what I presumed to be information cascaded down its length. The Eeri were a reclusive species, even after first contact had been made. They shared very little and refused to allow xenologists or ambassadors on their worlds or their ships. When negotiations were held between the trade branch of the Eeri, the Goldsmith Consortium, and the Telt, resulting in the construction of Kel Station—now known as the former StarBase 9.2—the Eeri had refused to send any of their own people to aid in the construction. If my understanding of that piece of history was correct, the Eeri provided a generous amount of credits but very little else.

The known worlds didn't even have a solid understanding of their linguistic systems, either. During the Cricade Wars, decryption programs relied heavily on AI translation work to help fill in the holes. And their medical capabilities were a wormhole of hot gossip and whisper net enthusiasts.

"The Error will remain still during deconstruction."

I thought I was. And despite my usual personality and the panic coursing inside me, I complied, all because of that pesky little word. I was determined to survive.

The information continued to appear on the screen, and I focused on that to stay calm. Symbols I presumed were their written language materialized, plus a series of information broken up into several groupings. *Well, Jupiter's moons. I bet I know what that is—my genome. The Eeri are looking at my genetic makeup. Oh. Well, scuttle crabs. And they're calling me an Error. If that wasn't some kind of mistranslation, then it didn't bode well. I wish Sam was here. I bet she'd be able to figure it out.*

<Mahia, we're being moved. Or at least forced somewhere. The dimensions of our cell shifted, and—>

<Shifted?>

<Yes,> Cain responded. *<It's like a long corridor we're being made to walk through. We can't refuse because the wall behind us continues to close in and push us forward. Wait, I think I see—>*

<Cain?>

"The Error will remain still. The Purified await the reaping."

The screen faded away, as did the lights.

<I don't know where we are. But we're okay. I think it's some kind of small shuttle, and it appears to be on autopilot.>

My adrenaline spiked. I didn't like being separated from Cain, and knowing he'd not been too far away had been comforting. But if they moved them into some kind of shuttle, I couldn't know where they were taking him. Our connection was a liability. If we were too far away from each other for too long, we would face consequences. And I wasn't liking what I was hearing, mistranslations or not.

The wall I was facing dissolved, and in front of me stood three robed figures—tightly woven dark-blue robes, to be exact. *Fudge nuggets.*

10

That's not Edible Tech

My first thought was that Yilmaz had pulled a bait-and-switch. Somehow, she'd tricked us. The three figures lifted their arms to pull back their hoods, and I cringed, ready for that all-shining light. But nothing blazed out from underneath the robes, and I breathed a small—very tiny—sigh of relief that Yilmaz hadn't betrayed us. *Yet,* I reminded myself.

After a series of clicks and whistles came a distorted version of the words "The Error will submit for the Purified."

Looking at what or, rather, who stood before me, I was confident I was facing the Eeri. The whisper nets were overrun with theories about the species, and there I was—just little old me—face-to-face with them. I recalled that wormhole about the medical side of things with this species. *Well. Here we go.*

Two theories existed. The first was that a collective of species came together and called themselves the Eeri. The second, more popular within academic circles, was that the Eeri genetically engineered different subspecies of themselves. And the academics weren't the only ones to run with that idea.

The whisper nets were full of rampant gossip and hotheaded debates, not to mention all the supposed eyewitness accounts from the Cricade Wars and the delegations who worked with the trade branch of the Eeri before the Brushe Conflict. That was where drone theories came in, but I never paid much attention to those, to be honest. You could bet your shiny rockets that I wished I'd done a lot more hardcore research about those guys, but my crystal ball never told me I'd be meeting them face-to-face one day. *What is it they say? Hindsight is twenty-twenty?*

Three pairs of unblinking eyes watched me.

"Hello?" I said with a small wave.

The Eeri standing in the middle clicked their beak and shook their head, their feathers briefly fluffing up before lying back down. "A modification level two is commanded."

"I apologize for the miscommunication, but I don't understand what you're asking of me. We don't have much time to hash it out, either. Is there some kind of translation program or tech we can use?"

All three Eeri clicked their beaks at me. *I'll take that as a no, then.*

The wall behind the Eeri abruptly shifted and was squished down into the shape of a corridor. From that, a strange hulked-up version of the Eeri standing before me appeared. It sported flesh, of a sort. Where its skin was visible, it had a strange green tint, and where its mouth should have been, was a beak. A row of feathers ran from the center of its forehead back to the base of its skull. One arm was definitely human, while the other looked like it had more in common with a Glipglow.

That one wore not a robe but a loose-fitting shirt-and-trousers combo, with the pants legs short enough to reveal two very birdlike feet with very sharp-looking talons. It bowed toward the three Eeri with a low whistle, and when it straightened, it clasped its hands—the humanoid hand had a wicked-looking talon in its pinkie finger.

"I am known as Woj-tu, of modification level two, of the Broken. You are to submit for the Purified." Despite its beak for a mouth, its speech was clear. But if the idea was to help bridge the communication gap, that wasn't working.

"Yeah, um… hello. So here's the deal. We're running out of time, and we need help figuring out—"

"You are the Error?" Woj-tu interrupted.

"I mean, I suppose. It's not a term I've ever used to describe myself before. I'm not really picking up on the context here, though. But the larger picture is that—"

"You have established connections with those of the Celestial Plain?"

I blinked. "Um, yes?" *Please don't blow me up—or anything else.* I was eyeing those nefarious-looking talons.

"Then you are required to submit." When I opened my mouth to politely protest, Woj-tu raised a hand. "An Error must submit for the Purified to declare their intentions of genetic reabsorption."

Yeah, no. "Let's say we've got a couple of options in front of us. Option A is that we came here because we thought the Eeri would have information regarding the Star Eaters. We've got a situation and could really use the help. Option B is whatever you're trying to ask me to do. And let's just say I'm really leaning toward Option A, just a friendly sit-down chat. With all of us. I'd really like to see my crew I came with." I eyed the corridor stretching out behind my hosts. *Maybe I can make a run for it.*

"The Error must submit."

"See, that's where we've got a problem. I've had people tinkering with my genetics for a little while now, and I'm over that. Where is the crew I came with?" I figured if I could get them to focus on a different topic, maybe we could take the whole idea of genetic reabsorption off the table.

"The guests of the Eeri are being shunted to more appropriate surroundings. The Error must submit."

That brief distraction certainly didn't last long. *<Cain? Still there?>* I sensed him, but if he was trying to answer, I couldn't hear him. *Great, just great.*

"Can you at least promise that there are some different ideas over the definition of the word reabsorption? That you will not kill me or something?"

Woj-tu blinked. "A blood debt is not required."

<Cain, if you can hear me, just know that I love you. And I'm trying to do what's right.>

"Are you sure we can't just all sit down and have a little chat?" When I didn't receive a response, I let out a long sigh, realizing I had survived some pretty strange things lately. *Alright, universe, let's see if my luck still holds.*

"Can you at least tell me if the Eeri are going to help us? Or if they even can?"

Woj-tu turned toward the three robed Eeri, but when they didn't respond except with their horrible unblinking gaze, he turned back toward me.

I bounced on my toes a couple of times, seriously considering making a mad dash for it, but the idea was ludicrous. I was fairly certain I could continue asking questions until I was blue in the face but wouldn't get any answers. *How in the worlds did I end up here?*

"How does the Error submit?" I asked.

"An Error must submit to the Purified through the transference made transcendent between the Mother of All and the Hatched."

This is how war breaks out between species. "I'm hearing the words you're saying, but I don't have a cultural framework to understand what they mean. You're going to have to give me step-by-step instructions here."

I'm not sure why, but a spark of understanding appeared in Woj-tu's eyes. *Finally.*

"You will kneel before the Purified."

Okay, universe. You'd better let me live through this.

"You will tilt your head back and open your mouth."

I frowned. "Excuse me?"

"You will tilt your head back and open your mouth."

Despite being a fool who'd eaten a piece of edible tech without knowing the consequences, I wasn't inclined to do something that idiotic again. "I mean no offense, truly, but I'm going to have to take a hard pass—"

The Eeri in the middle squawked—I know that's not a graceful term—and turned to glare at Woj-tu, who hissed and tilted their head to one side. Before I had time to react, Woj-tu was behind me and, with a rather convincing twist of my arm, had me on my knees. Then with their other hand, they grabbed the underside of my jaw to tilt my head back. That nasty-looking talon pressed against my jugular.

"The Error must submit to the Purified."

I didn't like my choices. If I struggled, that talon would hit its mark. *And bye-bye, me.* If I stayed still, I didn't know what nasty things would happen. *Maybe it's just some kind of DNA swab or something, just to confirm what their tech was showing them. That has to be it. Let's go with that.*

Nope of all the nastiest nopes in existence.

The Eeri in the middle stepped forward and leaned over me. They closed their eyes for a moment then opened them to stare at me. When they opened their beak, I realized what was up. As Woj-tu held me in place, something warm and sour coated my mouth. I coughed, and my stomach rolled.

"The Error must remain still."

I couldn't stop coughing, automatic gag reflexes being a hard thing to try to override. Woj-tu held me in place as I felt a too-horrible-to-even-try-to-name liquid slide down my throat. One of his hands moved from the side of my head to close my mouth, ensuring everything stayed in place. *Whoever thought of coming to these cloud suckers for help needs to be kicked out an airlock… Oh, wait. That was me. What joy.*

After the initial horrible few minutes—which I never want to go through again—my stomach settled down, and I felt okay. Better than okay—I felt great, all warm and fuzzy inside.

Woj-tu released me and helped me to my feet.

I giggled. "Now what?"

"The Error will be transferred until the time of Hatching."

I giggled again. I couldn't help it. "I hope it's somewhere warm and cozy. I could do with a little nap. Just curl up under a bundle of blankets and fall asleep."

Somewhere, a small part of my rational mind was screaming at me. Or maybe it was Cain.

But I heaved a sigh and leaned on Woj-tu for support. "Lead the way."

We walked past the three Eeri and down the long corridor, which continued to stretch forward until it stopped abruptly. I was having a hard time keeping my eyes open, but I glimpsed what looked like the exact opposite of where I expected an advanced civilization like the Eeri to live.

"Wow, what is this…" My words turned into mush, and I promptly fell asleep.

11

Pesky Family Trees

"Cain, she's waking up."

"Miles?" I asked.

"Yup. Hold on. He's coming. Here, let me help you sit up."

<I'm here. I've got you.>

Hands slipped under my shoulders and helped me scoot into a sitting position.

I rubbed at my eyes, trying to clear the grit, and licked my lips. "I could use something to drink."

"Not yet, I'm afraid. They gave us instructions. You're not to have any food or drink for the next three hours."

"Why?" I asked, turning my head as the room and a few concerned faces came into focus.

Miles frowned and glanced at Cain. "Something about a hatching," he mumbled.

"A hatching?" I asked, wishing my mind would clear.

Cain rushed his next question over mine. "How are you feeling?" He sat down next to me, running his hands over my body, double-checking for injuries.

"Other than being parched, I'm fine, I guess. Care to fill me in?"

Cain leaned back. "We were brought here and told to wait. And that you would join us after something they kept calling the… purification."

Oh, right… Ugh. The memory of what had happened resurfaced. *Maybe I shouldn't be too keen on wanting to know what was going on.* "I'm not sure I'd call it that," I mumbled, involuntarily wiping my mouth.

"Lie still." The Master Glipglow ran a claw down the length of my face, checking my biosigns.

"A bit like déjà vu, eh?" I joked, but no one laughed with me.

"Well?" Cain asked with a decidedly unhappy swish of his tail.

"We are still compiling the data that was provided," the master said.

Miles leaned over and asked the master a question—Cain was on high alert—but I ignored the chatter between the three of them. I let my head fall back against the wall. Cain had said they'd been moved, but from what he'd described earlier, I wondered what the difference was. Our room was another cube, barely larger than the one I'd originally been taken to. *Definitely a tad bit jealous now. This one is definitely cozy.* Cushions were strewn about, and Yilmaz had propped herself up in a corner, gazing out through the transparent walls.

Beyond our—the word "prison" didn't feel quite right. *"Enclosure," perhaps?* I eventually settled on the word "room." Beyond the walls of our room was a desolate landscape. A strong wind swept across the land, sending clouds of red dirt swirling into the air. Dead trees peppered the view, their black bark giving off vibes of ancient sentinels standing as reminders of a horrific fire—definitely not a tourist attraction.

"Where are we?" I asked, interrupting the others.

Yilmaz answered. "The Eeri home world."

I pushed myself up, fighting the wave of dizziness that came with the abrupt maneuver, and walked over to where she was sitting. "Really? Are you sure? I didn't think they allowed outside visitors."

"They don't," Miles answered from behind me. "And you can speculate on that little tidbit all you want. We certainly have."

"What's that supposed to mean?" I asked.

Cain and the master had moved off to one side, and judging from Cain's irritation flowing through me, they were having a little tiff.

"In all the negotiations that have been conducted with the Eeri, no one," Miles said as he leaned against the glass, "and I mean no one, has ever set foot on the Eeri homeworld. Oh, different governments and spy organizations have sent their best operatives, along with a battery of satellites and various spy-craft tech. The best they could get were a few snapshots of the world before the Eeri found the tech. Or the spies.

"So, judging from what I know, and the commandant here, we can safely assume we're on the Eeri home world. But what do you think they're going to do? Give us a few welcome gifts and let us go? A species that has obviously kept this place a secret for eons?"

"Well, aren't you just a little ray of sunshine," I

muttered. But I understood. "It is what we wanted, to contact the Eeri."

Miles scowled. "I'm not debating that. But why here, of all places? You don't just throw open the doors of your secret lair, now, do you?"

"I don't know. You did, back on Epsilon's Station."

Miles's continued spiral into annoyance clued me in to how desperate he was feeling, an emotion I hadn't really seen in the would-be emperor as yet.

"What's really going on?" I asked quietly.

"I don't like cramped quarters," he snapped then took a deep breath. "Bad memories."

Jail time. I'd forgotten about that. "We've been through worse," I said, with a specific glance at Yilmaz.

Miles looked at her and shook his head. "The *Justus*? Nah. Would've figured that one out, eventually."

"Gee, thanks for making me feel all needed and whatnot." I rolled my eyes and got a small smile in response.

"Just had to see what you were made of is all," Miles said. He rolled his shoulders and turned his attention back to Yilmaz. "I am curious to know if this was a part of your plan."

Yilmaz looked at us and sneered. "Do you really think I'd leave everything in order to get stuck in this miserable place? That I'd just let the known worlds burn?"

"You're the one who subscribes to the notion of sacrificing the many for the good of the one. Did you think this was some kind of escape plan? That you'd get us to bring you here so you could hide out and wait for the damage to be done?" I countered.

Yilmaz's eyes blazed with fury, and she got to her feet. "Hide? You think I want to be hiding at a time like this? You have no idea what I believe or why I believe what I do. I've sacrificed my entire life, along with hundreds of lives of the agents under my command, in order to protect the known worlds from the one threat I knew was lurking out there, but everyone else either wanted to ignore it or see if they could twist it to their own advantage. But here you are, poor little Mahia Orion, sticking her nose where it doesn't belong and unleashing the one thing that could rip apart the known worlds for good."

Miles stepped between us, and Cain's hands wrapped around my arms. But neither of them needed to have bothered.

"Don't you think I know that?" I hissed. "I'm the one who screwed up. And if the Eeri can't come through for us, or won't, then I get it. Everything that happens is my fault."

"It isn't your fault," Miles countered and threw a warning look at Yilmaz. "None of it is. If we'd all been truthful with you from the start, then perhaps none of this would've happened. Maybe we could've worked together. But if anyone should take blame, it's Yilmaz and myself. But not you, Mahia. All you've done is try to help."

"But isn't that the problem?" I asked and shook Cain off. I didn't have much space to stomp off, but I did my best. "If the Eeri don't help us, then what? Are we just going to sit here and twiddle our thumbs?"

"We're all on edge right now. What we need to do is calm down," Cain told the group. "We need to gather our intel and reassess our situation. Mahia, what happened with the Eeri?"

I glared at him. *<Mr. Know It All.>* But he was right, and I was embarrassed by my outburst. I thought I'd been moving beyond those things. *Chalk it up to the tension running through all of us.* "Nothing. Besides calling me an error and something about purification. They knew I hooked up with the Celestial Plain, though. But when I asked about them helping, they didn't respond."

"An error?" Miles asked.

I shrugged. "Who knows? Everyone's been screwing around with my genetics."

"Not screwing around but repairing and rearranging," the master corrected. "The tests that have been run confirm this."

"And I'm hearing a *but* in all of that," I said. "What are you hinting at?"

"The data is not complete. We are confident we've compiled roughly ninety percent but are hesitant to finish our theory as it may be adjusted once all the data has been compiled."

Tack on a few more pages of carefully worded indemnification clauses, and I'll be right at home. "Tell me anyway," I demanded.

"No. We wait until the master is sure," Cain said.

I narrowed my eyes and gave him a hard look. "And what does that mean, exactly?" *<What do you know that I don't?>*

"Nothing," Cain said, refusing to look me in the eye.

<Is this what you two were arguing about?>

"Do you wish us to proceed?" the master asked, patient and unruffled by the battle of wills between me and Cain.

"Yes," I said as Cain said, "No."

"Yes," I reiterated. "Whatever it is can't be as bad as what's already happened."

Miles and Yilmaz had gone quiet and stayed still, which was smart, considering the tension building between Cain and me.

"Mahia, let the master work. We need further information before jumping to conclusions. One misstep, and everything could come crashing down," Cain tried to reason.

I took a step forward and poked him in the chest. "I think we're beyond missteps. Everything is already falling apart, if you haven't noticed. And now, we're stuck on the Eeri home world. Their home world, for Jupiter's sake! I don't know how much worse it could get." *<Whatever pain you think you might be protecting me from, don't. I thought we were supposed to do this together.>*

<We are. But—>

<No buts.> I turned to the master. "Tell me."

The master blinked and snapped his lower jaws.

"Our original analysis was correct. There are segments of your DNA that are being rewritten, but not as we first suspected, with the working theory it was changing you into something new. A way for the Star Eaters—or what you've explained as the Third—to connect with you on a biological level." He stopped and appeared agitated. "Our apologies. This is where our understanding isn't confirmed. *Rewritten* is not the correct term. *Repaired* or *refurbished* may be better translations."

I wasn't sure I agreed with the master on that point. "Go on."

"The databases we keep have samples from billions of specimens—multiple species, multiple generations. We maintain a significant database dedicated to human biology as well. We are well versed in understanding the implications of what you term mitochondrial DNA. With the analysis we've conducted, we've noted that the smart-bots and the Third targeted these areas of your genetic makeup and are refurbishing these areas." His lower jaw opened and closed a few times, and his two pairs of hands clasped together into a tangled knot of talons. "If you recall, we mentioned having found similarities between what we've been monitoring in your DNA with information in our databases with an old trading partner. While we hesitate to fully commit to this theory, all of our preliminary results—coupled with an extrapolation of the terminology you've used, hatching and purification—indicate that on your maternal side, you have Eeri ancestry."

I stared at the Glipglow, and even if I'd tried to stop myself, I don't think I could've. I laughed—a lot—until I had to wipe tears from my face. But when I looked around the room, no one was laughing with me.

"You're not serious. Tell me you're joking."

The master glanced at Cain.

"No." I shook my head. "There's no way. None of this has been hinting at anything remotely like that. I'm sorry, but you've got your wires crossed somewhere."

Unable to process that little bombshell, I turned and stared out into the dead expanse. Cain moved to stand next to me.

<You were right,> I told him. <I should've listened. We'll see what they have to say when the data is finished compiling. Or however that works for them.>

"How sure are you?" Yilmaz asked the master.

"We feel comfortable with an eighty-three percent certainty."

I whirled around. "So, see? Plenty of room for errors."

"It would make a certain amount of sense," Yilmaz mused, ignoring me.

"Really, and how's that?" I snapped. "When I was on Dar, they scanned me. I'm human. Nothing else. If there had been something else lurking inside me, don't you think they would've known about it? I mean, they're pretty fanatical about tracing lineages and all that stuff."

Cain shifted his weight. <You've shared most of what happened on Dar with me. When the Holy One showed you the lineages, did you see both paternal and maternal?>

<What does that—>

I stopped as the memory flashed through my head. A shaft of light had appeared, and within it I'd seen the images of people I knew. But it'd only been the Orion family tree, my paternal side.

<But why wouldn't they have caught that?>

<I don't know. I'm sorry.>

I huffed and looked at Yilmaz. "Fine. I'll bite. Why would that make sense?"

"Because the Eeri contacted the Star Eaters millennia ago. That's why we're here. As a Gatekeeper, I'd always been taught that the Eeri were the one species who'd had the most contact with the Star Eaters." She leaned forward and stared at me, eyes bright. "But this brings everything full circle and explains why your father did two things: marrying your mother and going to the Eeri during the war."

12

Should've Declined the Invitation

Did it, though?

That newfound revelation—potential revelation—put me on edge. If it'd been any other species, I would've been fine. I have nothing against learning I've got a bit of something else in there. In fact, as a kid, I dreamed about that sort of thing, waking up and finding out I was a long-lost relative of some far-flung species that needed me for some mysterious reason. *Which now hits too close to home. But the Eeri? Why does it have to be them?* All those years of hate and animosity directed at them weren't going to just vanish in a couple of months—or a few minutes after a revelation like that.

But it's going to have to, isn't it? How long am I going to stay stuck in these feelings? I loved learning about different cultures and their customs, so the Eeri shouldn't have been any different, but they'd been the convenient scapegoat for my fear and anger.

As much as I was loath to admit it, if Yilmaz was

being truthful—and that was a huge if—then yes, this all made sense. I knew Pops had married my mom because her genetics were "outside" of the little breeding program the Sun Worshipers had going on. And the master's theory explained why Mrs. Gol and the others had been against the marriage.

With their ridiculous ideas about genetic purity, they wouldn't have wanted to add a touch of something else. Thinking of that little old woman actually helped because I could imagine her horror-stricken look when Pops told her. And that made me quite happy.

I let my thoughts roll through the information and realized something else was nagging at me, details I knew had to be important but I couldn't pinpoint. Pushing those annoyances to the side, I focused on what was in front of me.

"Then what's this 'error' nonsense?" I asked. "Or 'hatching'? Any thoughts?"

Just as the master started to share his theories, the dimensions of our room shifted. The ceiling moved upward a few meters, and the space doubled in size. A narrow corridor appeared, and Woj-tu walked into our little cell.

Cain flung out a hand and tried to shove me behind himself.

<*Heroic, but unnecessary.*> I shoved him to one side and stepped out in front of him. <*I've already been introduced to this one.*>

Woj-tu bowed toward me. "I am Yul-wy, of modification level two, of the Broken. I am to escort you to the Halls of Disillusion. Please come with me."

Whoops, okay. So I hadn't met them. I wasn't off to a great start if I couldn't tell those guys apart.

When Yilmaz got to her feet and we all moved to follow Yul-wy, they held up a hand and shook their head. "The invitation has been presented for the Error. The rest of you are invited to relax and breathe in the air that is of the Shell."

"No. Where she goes, I go," Cain growled.

Yul-wy blinked and clicked their beak. "The invitation has been—"

I took a step toward Yul-wy and forced myself to bow. "I appreciate the invitation and accept, on the condition that I must insist that my crew comes with me."

Yul-wy blinked again then backed up into the corridor. Before any of us could do a thing, the corridor and its occupant vanished.

"Well, fudge nuggets," I muttered. "Now what?"

"We wait," Yilmaz said. "They're being rather gracious for an extremely reclusive species. And toward all of us. Which means we each must have value to them."

I rolled my eyes and huffed. *I wish Ochoa was here instead of you.* Then I cringed at the thought and desperately wished that Ochoa, Lio, and the rest of the *Samaritan* crew had survived or, if they'd been captured by the Jumjul, that we could fix this mess before they were transferred to a penal colony or worse. That made me wonder what the Jumjul were up to. *Will they come after us?* I shivered. The Jumjul were fanatical about order. I couldn't even consider a scenario that didn't involve them demanding justice for what had happened.

Thankfully, my thoughts along that line were

interrupted when Yul-wy—I assumed the Eeri was the same one—reappeared.

They bowed. "The invitation has been changed to include the Error and the guests of the Eeri. Please follow me."

Well, hot dog.

Cain tried to worm his way past me to the front, but I wouldn't have it. I did appreciate the gesture, but I needed to take the lead. He grumbled and mumbled a few unsavory things and gave up eventually. But if I'd had a tail, he would've been stepping on it continuously.

The corridor stretched out before us as we walked and moved at a slight downward angle. I couldn't help but wonder if the atmosphere was toxic for us or if a cultural taboo existed with other species on their planet. *But they said something about breathing the air.* Yul-wy led us past a grove of dead trees, each as pathetic looking as the last.

"What happened here? Can you tell us?" I asked, my curiosity getting the better of me.

The Eeri inhaled sharply, with a slight flutter of feathers. "We are moving through the Sundering, a reminder of the hubris of what the Shell believed in the Time Before."

"Can you expand on what the Sundering was?" Miles asked diplomatically.

"When the Shell learned the consequences of their touch within the galaxy."

Yul-wy stopped as we reached a dead end, and a circle of light appeared. They stepped to one side and motioned toward the light. "Please. One at a time."

"This isn't another deconstruction-type thing, is it?"
I half joked.

Yul-wy blinked and shook their head. "The Error has already begun deconstruction. This aids movement."

Begun? My brain got hung up on the word as Miles stepped into the light.

"Right, well, here goes nothing." He had just enough time for a wink, and he opened his mouth to say, "Some-one's got to be the—" Then, with a blink, he was gone.

"Where is he?" Cain growled.

"Please. One at a time."

Yilmaz came forward and turned to look at us. "We're allies right now because of what must be done. Believe me, this pains me as much as it's going to pain you. But I'm putting my trust in you two. Whatever happens, do whatever you must in order to stop the Star Eaters. Are we clear?"

I stared at her as she stepped into the light.

<Look, I don't like this any more than you do. But so far, they haven't outright rejected us or shot us. No one really understands these guys or what cultural customs they have. I'll see you on the other side.> I reached out and squeezed Cain's hand.

But he held fast and wouldn't let me go.

"No. Let me go first." He raised his other hand to stop me from arguing. "I know you don't need protec-tion—" *<For the most part. You have had some fairly dumb ideas.>* "But at least let me do this. Let me go first. And whatever is waiting for us on the other side, I can scout it out, at least."

I was tempted to shake my head and insist on going

first, but he had a point. He was still IGJ trained, and I wasn't. The smart move would be to let him go first.

"Fine," I said but caught the edge of his now ratty-looking uniform and pulled him close. "But be careful."

<Always.>

He stepped into the light and was gone.

"We will go next," the master said. "Hatchlings are to be protected at all costs." And without any other preamble, the master stepped into the light and vanished.

I glanced over at my escort, who was dutifully avoiding my gaze. *Well, I can't let them have all the fun.* I stepped into the circle of light and crossed my fingers.

Keeping them crossed, I stared in shock at where the transport tech took us. Wind ripped through a narrow hallway, and despite thick pillars lining both sides, it had a tangled web of branches instead of a traditional ceiling. Soaring high above us or peering down between the branches were dozens upon dozens of Eeri. Their eyes caught the light as they sent multiple sharp, piercing calls back and forth.

I craned my neck upward to watch as Eeri from the sky alighted onto the branches, feathered wings ruffling. A few of them vied for one perch or another. As the last Eeri settled, the wind died down, and I heard clicks and whistles among the last few cries.

While I was gaping at the Eeri, Cain and the others were forming a protective ring around me. I shifted my focus to the massive columns, noting each one had a vertical column of what I presumed was the Eeri's written language. But what stood between the massive columns really snagged my attention. At first, I assumed they were statues, but as I continued to stare, I realized I was wrong. *They weren't carved—they're preserved.* And each one was slightly different. A beak was visible here or there, feathers in different places, wings on some, and humanoid arms on others. On the other side, more had varying resemblances to the Eeri and a handful of other species I didn't recognize.

<What in the worlds is this?> I silently asked Cain.

<A bad feeling,> he replied and took a step closer. *<We need to get out of here.>*

Yul-wy cleared their throat. "The Error and guests are welcomed into the Hall of Disillusion. If the Error will follow..."

"She's not going anywhere," Cain said as he and Miles both stepped up in front of me. "We came here in good faith. And now we want to leave in good faith."

"You will be allowed to leave once the Error has been reclaimed. Proof of reclamation must be provided to the Jumjul High Court. Once submitted and accepted, the guests of the Eeri will be allowed to leave and await their judgment from the Jumjul High Court."

"Wait a minute. No one said anything about the Jumjul," Miles said.

Yul-wy blinked, appearing a tad flustered. "You will be allowed to leave once the—"

"We heard that the first time," Miles interrupted. "I demand to know on whose authority you're operating."

The feathers atop of Yul-wy's head rose, and the poor guy appeared to tremor. "Please wait here." With a bow and a click of their beak, Yul-wy turned and hurried down the hallway.

"Do you see any doors?" Cain asked.

"That wouldn't be wise," Yilmaz spoke up. "We're not alone. And I doubt they'd take kindly to any attempts to escape, despite their politeness up to this point."

"You're supposedly the expert," Cain snapped, whirling around to face Yilmaz. "Get us out of here, or else—"

"I never said I was the expert. I would caution against putting words in others' mouths," she replied calmly. The woman's ability to keep her cool in that type of situation was admirable. "I told you I've had dealings with the Eeri before, but through their usual communications, not anything like this. I used that and my status as a Gatekeeper to help you make contact. But as I'm sure you remember from your IGJ training, we know very little about the Eeri when it comes to their customs and cultural structure."

"Perhaps I can explain," a fresh voice entered the conversation.

I turned to see a distinctly human-looking figure standing behind us, and with a shock I don't think anyone could ever have prepared for, I realized that person was the spitting image of my mom.

13

Talons Galore

"Mahia?" Yilmaz asked, undoubtedly noting my swift intake of breath.

<What's wrong?> Cain stepped toward me as I stepped back.

"That's not possible," I said. "You're dead."

As a flutter of unrest ran through our audience above us, the woman bowed. "I apologize if this construct is unwelcome. They hoped a familiar face would ease the transition."

"A familiar face?" Cain asked then took a closer look. "Who are you?" he demanded.

"I am to be called Risa, a modification level three of the Broken. Would you wish us to choose another form?"

"No," I mumbled. "This is… fine. It's all totally fine. Peachy, in fact." I glanced at Cain and shrugged. *I mean, what's another blast from my past? First, dealing with the revelations about Pops, then Lucas, so why not her?* "This is—or, rather, looks exactly like—my mom."

For once, Cain gaped right along with me, as did Miles, judging from his silence on the matter.

The master seemed unfazed. "You are a construct from a genetic bank?" they asked.

"I am. I was created but left on standby in case there were… complications. The Eeri have learned it is best to approach those outside the Shell with forms that are familiar and comforting."

"Standby?" I croaked.

Risa nodded. "Yes. There was hope the reclamation process would be swift and all could return as it was. But as there appeared to be further breakdown, they sent me to facilitate the next steps and authorized me to provide explanations."

"And these"—the master waved an arm at the frozen figures between the columns—"these are the results of the Eeri conducting genetic experiments?"

"These you see before you are the exalted among the Broken, those who have served outside the Shell," Risa explained. At least, in her mind, she was explaining.

But understanding kicked in, and I shook my head. "You're telling me the Eeri genetically modify themselves to look like the species they're contacting?"

Risa nodded. "Yes. There was a significant… trial and error while the Purified developed a system for facilitating contact. Over time, the Broken were developed, each level genetically developed for appropriate levels of contact."

"Yeah, I was introduced to a few level twos, and you said you were, what, a level three?" I asked.

"Yes. Level threes are created to genetically mirror the species they are tasked with studying. That particular

Broken is sent out to gather information—cultural, religious, governmental—as much as they can.

"If the Eeri feel enough information has been obtained and they wish to proceed, a level one of the Broken is created. These physically imitate the Purified but are not of the Purified, for the harmony of the Shell must be maintained. But they have the authority to seek out the appropriate authorities to initiate contact through nonphysical means."

"And what about the level twos?" I asked, thinking of our two previous hosts.

"An amalgamation of useful physical attributes. 'Drones' might be an adequate translation, constructed for varying types of labor."

"But the level ones are more or less the Eeri or, rather, the Purified?" the master clarified.

Risa glanced up at the Eeri watching us. "Almost perfect genetic clones, but with slight modifications. Again, harmony must be maintained, and the Purified do not reveal themselves."

Wow. Who knew some of the whisper nets would be halfway right? But as fascinating as the information was, none of it answered the question literally staring me in the face.

"But how do you have a genetic sample of my mom?"

"It was a condition of the meeting between Wats Hawking Orion and the Purified."

Well, dammit. Pops, I thought we'd gotten everything sorted out, and now this. What the hell?

"The Broken who are sent out for first contact—what becomes of them?" the master continued to press.

Risa's polite expression faltered, but at least she didn't clam up. "They are reclaimed, allowing the Purified to maintain discretion in how they approach new species. But in some circumstances, breeding has occurred, and an Error has been created. The Purified do what they can in order to hunt and destroy these Errors, but many"—she glanced up and dropped her voice—"have evaded reclamation."

Clever. I didn't care for what she was implying, but I was right on the heels of what the master was thinking. "Are you saying my mom was… one of the Broken?" I asked.

Risa shook her head. "No. She was an Error, as was her foremother and the one before her. This… genetic line was kept hidden from us, and the Purified could not reclaim it, despite all attempts to do so. But an opportunity presented itself to rectify the situation, and the Purified—"

A screech tore through the grand hallway, and for a moment, I froze in terror and a smidgen of wonder as a handful of Eeri took to the air. Despite the prejudice I'd carried around for years, along with the misgivings I currently felt, the Eeri were beautiful to behold—until one of them swept over us, claws extended and barely missing Risa's head.

Risa paled, and her demeanor shifted. "A process which must be completed for the sanctity of the Shell. This horrible oversight must be corrected."

"We would be interested to learn of this reclamation process. What does it entail?" the master inquired politely.

Miles added, "This would help to ease our concerns and would be greatly appreciated."

A dramatic pause ensued as we waited for the answer. Cain was bouncing on his toes, his level of agitation about to explode. *<Remind me how you passed* IGJ *training,>* I said. *<Surely, there was a Keep Calm 101 course or something.>*

My jab broke his concentration, and I earned a snarl. But at least he stopped bouncing around.

"This can be allowed. If you would follow me," Risa finally answered. Without leaving room for any further discussion, she walked past us. The abrupt movement caused a memory to float loose, and I had the faintest impression of remembering looking up from a bed or a playpen of sorts as my mom walked past me and gave me a smile.

I reached out involuntarily, wanting to touch her arm, but snapped my hand back at the last second. Of course Cain would catch my little blunder. *<Wait a moment. Let them go first,>* he thought.

We hung back until the others were a few steps ahead of us.

<We'll find a way around all of this.> A rush of warmth and good intentions flowed behind his words, but he wasn't able to keep an undercurrent of fear from coming through also.

I wasn't sure if I was afraid. I didn't know what I felt. *Another round of betrayal from my family? Surely my mom would've known. If not, how did my pops figure it out?* With the access Pops had had to different organizations and databases—especially knowing how he'd been looking for something "genetically different" from what the breeding program was supplying—I had no doubt he'd been clever enough to figure it out.

Cain was waiting for a response, giving me a moment to process this latest revelation. But my mind was already moving off in a different direction. That nagging feeling of missing how everything was connected was back and was a lot more insistent.

I shooed Cain on. *<I'm fine. Let's just figure this out. Okay?>* I knew he didn't believe me, but he didn't protest, probably more because we had an attentive audience than because he'd decided not to stand his ground and push.

The length of the hallway was deceptive, and instead of taking a few minutes to walk down, it took ages. *Perhaps another type of tech, like the clear boxes and corridors that appeared. Or hologram-type tech. Nope—this isn't the time to speculate. Doesn't matter. Just focus.*

I looked at the Broken as we passed, noting an elegance to the forms I hadn't originally appreciated. The concept had merit, especially when contacting species not well versed in the plethora of life inhabiting the known worlds. And it did clue me in to one thing about the Eeri—they were patient. Years of trust would have to be built up between their representatives and whatever species they were working with, to avoid hurt feelings or mistrust when the truth was revealed.

While human physical traits were apparent here and there, Risa was the only one who appeared fully human. I racked my memory, trying to recall if I'd seen or heard anything that discussed initial human contact with the Eeri. I couldn't recall a blasted thing. The only thing I could conjure up was the agreements settled on before the Cricade War. And I thought I remembered something about the Telt bringing the Eeri to the table. Or maybe I was just making stuff up, trying to fit it in with what I was seeing. Pops might've educated his children on a wide range of topics and points of history, but no way could anyone learn it all.

As we kept walking quietly, I glanced at the next Broken and realized something else. They all had one thing in common. Draped around their shoulders was a blue robe.

"Wait," I said and stopped. The questions building up inside me had to come out. "Did the Eeri do all of this with humanity? I mean this whole first-contact deal with a Broken?"

"No," Risa replied.

Before she realized exactly how much information she'd given me with that one brief word, I pressed on. "What about the Star Eaters—or, rather, the Celestial Plain? Did the Eeri contact them?"

"Yes."

Gotcha. "Then I need you to explain something for me. If the Eeri didn't create Broken in order to initiate contact with humanity, then how was my mother an Error? Or me? How did we end up with Eeri DNA?"

Risa pursed her lips. "This information is unavailable."

I slowly made my way through our little group. "Unacceptable. You're going to make that information available or get permission from whoever or whatever you need to. Your reclamation and the Jumjul High Court be damned. We came here to fix something that

I did, but I'm getting the feeling this is an Eeri problem as well. So cough it up."

"Perhaps this isn't the best way to continue to get their cooperation," Miles quietly cautioned.

"It might not be, but if there was ever a time for your madman routine and not the would-be emperor, this is it. The Star Eaters are destroying one solar system. How long until they move on?" I turned to Yilmaz. "You've said the known worlds are in peril. So that means not just one system, but *all* the systems."

She nodded but didn't add anything.

"This information is still unavailable," Risa said. "Please follow me." She glanced up at our watchful hosts. "We're running out of time."

"No."

To my shock, the word didn't come from me but from Yilmaz. In that moment, the woman earned just a tidge of a touch of respect from me. Her movements and reflexes were lightning quick, and before any of us could blink, she was behind Risa, an arm wrapped around her neck.

"I am Commandant Hazine Umtholopali Yilmaz, Scion Prime and Gatekeeper of Lo-Liopath-Poli. You will answer our questions, or else I am within my rights to terminate you."

Miles and Cain reacted, taking defensive postures on either side of Yilmaz. Conflict erupted in my brain. *That's not my mom. No matter what she looks like, that's not my mom.* I had absolutely no obligation to her.

Cries of outrage filled the hallway, and the Eeri took to the air. I tilted my head back, weary but ready. While the majority settled back down on the twisted web of branches, five of them landed and formed a circle around us. They had cleverly crafted their thick blue robes to allow freedom of movement both in the air and on the ground. Each one pulled back their hood, and their razor-sharp beaks clicked in anger.

The master let off a rumble of thunder, and his lower jaws opened wide, rows of razor-sharp teeth glinting in the light. With a snap, crackle, and pop, his talons blazed brightly. *Jupiter, I didn't think those things really existed.* Rumors, even among the Weplies, talked about Glipglow talon tech that could cut through anything.

"We didn't come here for a fight. We came here for your help—help you gave my pops several years ago. I want to understand why, to understand this entire mess I've made." I corrected myself. "*We've* made, evidently."

I moved past the master and marched up to the nearest Eeri, not flinching or backing down. Everything was on the line. Ochoa's caution made me pause, but only for a fraction of a second.

"But if we have to fight in order to get what we need, then so be it."

The Eeri leaned forward, its beak millimeters away from my face. Up close, I caught a shimmer of iridescence off the small feathers fanning out between its eyes. I smelled a faint odor of fish and something floral as well. *Can it, xenologist wannabe. Not a time for wormholes.*

My heart was ready to burst from the anxiety, and beads of sweat were forming on my forehead, ready to roll down and give away my absolute terror.

<You will duck. Clear?>

<Clear.>

I took in a deep breath, not breaking eye contact, ready to do what had to be done if the Eeri didn't back down. And from behind me came what I can only describe as a war cry.

<Now!>

My up-close-and-personal Eeri pulled back with an earsplitting cry as it lifted a shoulder and shrugged off its robe, revealing an impressive array of weapons tucked between soft yellow and orange feathers.

<Duck! Do it now!>

I ducked, and something leaped over me in a blur of green and scales. I heard the horrific sound of jaws snapping shut as the master broke the Eeri's neck as he sliced through their body. My brain shut down. It had to in order to survive. We were no longer fighting living creatures but monstrous constructs.

A pair of hands grabbed me from behind, pulling me back with such force that I slid across the floor to land at Yilmaz's feet. She, in turn, threw me a bracelet while keeping her hold on Risa.

"Really?" I asked as I scrambled to my feet and slid it over my hand. "How in the worlds did you smuggle this in?"

Yilmaz threw me a wicked grin. "Wasn't me. Ask your madman over there."

Good old Miles—should've known.

The Vulture tech sprang to life, and I primed the weapon, taking stock of the situation. I glanced up, noting the Eeri on the ledges, calling back and forth, hopping around in agitation and excitement. *Oh goodie. A ring fight—one they think they're going to win.*

Despite the odds not being on our side, the master had already made quick work of one Eeri and was fighting a second. That one had learned the lesson: stay clear of those nasty talons.

Cain was fending off two Eeri, spinning and darting out of the way of powerful wings and razor-sharp claws.

<Set one of them up,> I told him.

Cain hopped to one side and ducked as a wing swept forward to knock him down. I lifted my arm and fired—a clean shot through the center of the wing. The Eeri cried out in pain, and I took aim again and fired. After that, it was silent.

Cain took advantage of the momentary confusion with the second Eeri and leaped onto its back. As the Eeri toppled to the floor, Cain jumped down and moved to help Miles, but by the time he reached him, Miles had used his own smuggled weapon and electrocuted the Eeri.

I made a hasty assumption that what I'd interpreted as cheers and jeers had turned into calls of absolute outrage.

Yilmaz took charge and hollered, "Miles, provide cover! You, Master, clear the path in front of us. Cain, protect Mahia. Move!"

The Eeri were swarming then, and a few flew down, their feet spread open, ready to rip through us. Miles took aim, and a spark of electricity arced through the sky and hit its mark. The Eeri beside it pulled up just in time, its wings pumping furiously and its scream of rage ripping through the air.

Risa was struggling against Yilmaz and gasped, "No. Stop, turn. Here, now… go here!" She raised a hand and pointed at one of the Broken. "The Purified won't follow us."

I glanced up at the darkening cloud of Eeri ready to rip us to shreds. *We just started our own little personal war. Great.* I looked back at Risa, the Eeri construct with the face of my mom. *Do we dare trust her?*

But I knew if we stayed, we would die. Too many Eeri were there, and we'd lost the element of surprise. Even if we made it back to the transporter, we had no way to activate it, let alone configure it to travel somewhere safe. But on the slim chance that Risa was telling us the truth, then perhaps we could make it. Perhaps we could regroup and find a defensible position, at least. *Alright, it's go time.*

"Do it!" I shouted.

Yilmaz obviously felt the same, as she released Risa, and we raced after her, slipping between a Broken and a column, leaving the screeches of outrage behind.

14

Piggyback Rides

We raced down a dimly lit corridor and followed Risa as she made an abrupt left turn. Eventually, we made too many turns to remember. Yilmaz remained in the lead, ready to react if Risa tried anything funky, with Cain hot on her heels, while I was slowing down. My adrenaline dump during the fight was rapidly fading. Miles slowed to match my pace, and the master guarded us from the rear. I couldn't help but glance over my shoulder a few times as we ran into the unknown, each time sure I would see a flock of enraged Eeri coming after us. But each time, nothing was there but darkness stretching out behind, along with the sound of our feet pounding against the floor.

By the time Risa finally came to a stop, my lungs felt like they were going to burst. She was barely showing any signs of wear after that little marathon. I felt a tad jealous.

"They won't follow. But the level two of the Broken will be activated. We don't have much time," Risa told us.

Despite gasping for breath, I marched over to her

and shoved her up against the wall. "Why are you help-ing us?"

"Because I'm like you," Risa calmly answered.

I couldn't help but laugh between a few coughs. "No, you're not. You're nothing but a genetic clone, something grown in a lab." *You're not my mom. You're not human. You're a construct.*

A brief look of sorrow crossed Risa's face before she caught herself. "That may be, but the Purified have perfected the art of cloning, down to grafting what you might call genetic memory into the Broken. They con-sider it efficient, not having to provide training or hours of updates for each level of the Broken. Preprogrammed workers, you might say."

My arm at her throat suddenly felt hot to the touch, and I flew back. "No. Maybe that's something unique to the Eeri, but don't you dare imply you have the mem-ories of my—"

"We don't have time to debate. You're running out of time. And options," Risa said as she straightened her jacket. "But like it or not, I contain all the memories of your mother and those before her."

"Even if what you say is true, having those mem-ories doesn't automatically move you into my circle of trust. So, answer my question," I snapped. "Why are you helping us?"

Cain moved to my side, placing a hand on my elbow, and I leaned against him for support.

Risa took a deep breath. "I can tell you once we're safe."

"No," Cain growled. "You tell her now, or else you won't be going anywhere."

"An unwise choice of action, if you truly want to stop the Star Eaters. The Purified won't help you, not again. Wats broke his promise, and now, it appears you will too."

"Excuse me?" I said.

"Enough," Yilmaz said. "Why is she running out of time?"

"The process of reabsorption is nearly complete. If we wish to stop this, we must hurry."

Oh yeah. No wonder I feel so lousy. Forgot that little snag. "What did they do to me?"

"They are stripping your body of genetic material they consider inherited from the Errors."

I was pretty sure I knew what that meant but looked over at the master, who didn't need to say anything at all, just nodding. *Well, fudge.*

But Miles wasn't following. "And what does that mean, exactly?"

"What do you do with tech that malfunctions?" I asked Miles. "I can tell you. You reclaim it. Maybe break it down into parts that can be useful. And if not, then it's destroyed."

"Surely you're not suggesting…" Miles started.

I laughed, cold and hard. "Don't tell me the great Miles High is suddenly squeamish. You wouldn't hesitate to make sure someone that wasn't up to snuff in your organization was taken care of."

"The Purified will do what is necessary, as they have done for generations," Risa said stiffly. "An Error of your genetic material cannot be abided. Not now. Not after what Wats refused to do or what you've done."

What Pops refused to do? Then the truth smacked me in the face. *Pops let me live. He let Lucas live. He kept working on figuring out what the Sun Worshipers had been after for so many generations.* "Right, because I'm a huge red flag for anyone who can put the pieces together about what the Eeri did," I countered.

"I'm not following you," Cain said softly.

"She told us that the Eeri never contacted humans, but they made contact with the *Celestial Plain* or, rather, the Two, whom we've been calling the Star Eaters. And let's not forget those blasted blue cloaks the Star Eaters wear, exactly like what we just saw the Eeri wearing. Plus, when I was on the *Rapscallion* and the Star Eaters rescued me from Mrs. Gol, they spoke with a series of clicks and whistles but could also speak Standard—languages they'd learned or had been taught," I said.

I turned and looked at Yilmaz. "Throughout the years, the reports about Star Eater activity have really been about the Star Eater *cult*—all the skirmishes and dustups with those strange creatures in blue robes. But we've learned that there are actually only *two* true Star Eaters—the Two of the Celestial Plain. And so, all those other mysterious robed figures who've been wreaking havoc throughout the known worlds? Strange shapes and biosigns, where no one could pin down which species they might be?"

Yilmaz's eyes lit up like an old-fashioned Christmas tree. "The Errors."

I nodded. "Exactly." I turned back toward Risa. *<If*

this next place doesn't pan out, we find our own way,> I told Cain. *<This is feeling a little too much like being led on a wild goose chase.>*

<A wild what?>

<Goose. Don't you know what those are?>

Cain shook his head.

<Alright. You know what, if we make it out of this alive, I'm taking you to the Lunar History Zoo.>

Cain grinned. *<Deal.>*

Yilmaz motioned to the master. "If you don't mind?"

The master nodded and moved to guard Risa, while Miles joined us for a little huddle.

"We have very few options at the moment," Yilmaz said quietly. "Normally, I wouldn't advise trusting someone I haven't vetted. But given the circumstances, our chances of making it out of here on our own are slim to none. We don't have enough intel about the Eeri home world. And frankly, Mahia, you won't make it without help, something we can't provide you with right now."

<She's right, as much as I'm loath to admit it,> Cain added. *<At least we can be prepared if we're walking into a trap. And Risa might be the way to get the information we need.>*

<And how do we know this isn't one of Yilmaz's games? Or a trap of her own making?> I countered.

Miles jumped in before Cain replied. "And whatever slight chance existed of getting the Eeri to not turn us over to the Jumjul is certainly gone. My guess is that they'll be here any moment. The *Samaritan*"—Miles choked up a bit—"bought us time, but not days. Hours, at best. The Jumjul are going to be fanatical about seeking justice, not to mention the Eeri had already thrown their lot in with the Jumjul over Lucas's idiotic maneuvers. Now, they've got even more reason to do so."

"Not to mention the inbound Glipglows," I added. "What side will they fall on once they've secured the master?"

Cain had been watching Yilmaz, and I sensed reluctance and self-disgust as he straightened up and looked her in the eye. "Yilmaz is right. Our options are sorely limited. If we're going to make it through this"—he squeezed my hand—"or at least meet our original objective of finding a way to stop the Star Eaters, then we play along for now. But with our eyes open for anything or anyone who might betray us."

<Are you sure?> I asked.

Cain nodded. *<Yes. She's right—we don't know how to help you. But Risa might.>*

"Alrighty then." I turned toward Risa. "You said you wouldn't talk until we were safe. Well? Show us the way."

The master stepped off to one side, allowing Risa to take the lead once more. We followed her down the corridor until the walls stopped shifting, and we came to a dead end. A shaft of light appeared in front of us.

"We'll transport out of the Halls of the Broken," she said. "There is a place we've maintained separate from the Purified. You'll be safe there."

"We?" Cain asked.

"Yes. Those of us who have been working outside of the Purified." Without any further explanation, Risa stepped into the light and vanished.

After a moment of hesitation among our little group,

the master moved through us and stepped into the light, then one by one, we followed.

I blinked and opened my eyes to stare at a desolate landscape similar to what we'd seen in the cube. Barren hills stretched out before us, with clusters of dead and burned-looking trees. The air was still and gave me the creeps. Risa was waiting for us and beckoned us to follow. I caught Miles asking the master about air quality but didn't catch the reply. But when Miles didn't appear worried, I decided to not be concerned as well.

Not long thereafter, I had to sit down. My breaths were shallow, and each one hurt. Cain squatted down next to me, unchecked worry clear in his eyes.

I reached out for him. "I just need to catch my breath, is all."

A shadow fell across us as the master approached. "Hatchlings are to be protected at all costs. Come." He knelt.

After a few moments, I realized what he was offering. A part of me wanted to politely refuse. No way was carrying me dignified, for either of us. But the pain in my chest wasn't going away, and judging by the lack of anything helpful nearby, we still had a ways to go.

"Are you sure?" I asked.

"Yes."

Cain helped me settle on the master's back, and I leaned my head between his shoulders as the upper two arms rotated back and held me in place. *Well, isn't that nifty? Extra joints. Who would've known?*

We followed Risa across the hills for what felt like

hours. The twin suns had reached their zenith and did their best to melt us into puddles of goo.

<I don't know how much more of this the master can take. They've got to be getting tired. Plus hungry. I'm hungry, so they've got to be as well, right?>

"When are you ever not hungry?" Cain asked as he kept pace beside the master.

I halfheartedly tried to laugh, but *wheezed* would be a more accurate description. "There's plenty of times I'm not. But seriously, how much longer can we go on? And we're out in the open too. Exposed."

"Actually, I don't think we are," Cain replied cryptically.

"What?"

"Come on, aren't you the expert tech person?" he teased.

I narrowed my eyes. "I'm in no mood for guessing games." But when he gave me a smug look in response, I huffed in frustration and tried to figure out what in the worlds I was missing.

I turned my head and watched Cain kick at a rock. It flew off to one side amid puffs of dirt. Everything looked solid beneath his feet. No telltale glimmer of tech obscured my view, no matter which way I looked.

"Look up," Cain said finally.

I had already, but the suns were bright and made me squint. I lifted a hand to shield my eyes. "Son of a—"

"If we weren't on the brink of war with these guys, I would negotiate some trade agreements. Pretty damn sophisticated," Miles interjected. "My best guess is some type of shielding tech that's moving with us, and Risa's carrying the transmitter. But there's a level of engineering that's brilliant."

"They'd have to have mapped either the exact route we're taking, or the entire area. Or it's working with a real-time broadcast system," I said, "high res with no hiccups, or else our location would be a dead giveaway. Not to mention thermal HalfLife biochips and masking for any other types of scanning or tracking tech."

Miles nodded. "Yup. Think how handy this would be in my operations."

"We are aware of a master who would be delighted to work with you on an approximation of this technology," the master interjected.

I couldn't help but feel a little lift of my spirits as a huge, boyish grin spread across Miles's face. Then he was off, discussing the legalities of such a collaboration.

<That's more like it.>

<What?> I asked.

<Seeing you smile.>

<Not much to smile about. This isn't a vacation I'd book again. I almost wish we were back on the Starshine.*>*

Cain chuckled but remained silent. I appreciated not being hounded with questions about how I was feeling because even I wasn't sure how I was, emotionally. Even after all the surprises and mixed-up adventures one little old vacation voucher had landed me in, seeing my mom—a genetic clone of my mom at least—was decidedly not an event I would have anticipated in a gazillion years. *Of course, universe, just after I did so much work to make peace over what Pops and Lucas had gotten up to, you just have to throw in this kind of wrinkle.*

"You know what?" I blurted out. "It's just like we've talked about before."

Cain raised an eyebrow at me.

"I'm not responsible for Pops or Lucas's actions, and neither am I responsible for anything my mom might have done. The truth is she's more of a mystery figure in my memories than anything real or tangible like Pops or Lucas." I loved the idea of a mother and had good memories of the little I could recall before she died.

My attention turned to Risa leading us, and I realized that even though she might wear the face of the memory I had of my mom, she decidedly wasn't her, no matter what genetic memory programming might've happened. *<My mom died years ago, and she loved Pops and he her. That's what matters.>*

"Speaking of moms," I said, "what do you think yours is doing? Surely she's gotten the message by now."

Cain shrugged. "Any number of things. I'm confident she'll take the note seriously, but depending on the IGJ response and the current political climate…"

"You don't think she'll try to get the word out? Wasn't that the whole point of alerting her?"

"Yes, she will. But how she does that will depend on the current political situation. She knows how to play the game, and she does it extremely well. All of this could be used to maneuver her into new—"

"We're here," Risa called.

Right… I looked around, and absolutely nothing looked different until Risa reached out and tapped the air, which appeared to ripple outward as if she'd touched a still body of water. In the center of the ever-expanding ripples, a break in the landscape appeared, revealing a small, rough hut constructed from dead branches and covered in some type of crude coating.

She beckoned us to step into the hut, and surprise, surprise, another zap 'n' roll happened. I really hoped they'd worked out the kinks on the whole molecular damage issue.

15

A Giant Leap of Faith

We stepped into a bustling marketplace. Rather, we stepped into a bustling marketplace surrounded by guards with spears and lances aimed at us.

"What is this?" I hissed. "We trusted you."

Risa raised a hand. "I haven't broken my word. But we must ensure any tech you're carrying can't be traced. Please allow Lunna to inspect you."

A tall, strange mixture of Eeri and Telt stepped into view. Above her beak, fur spread up and across her forehead, but instead of a hairline it was a feather line. Bright-yellow feathers made a strange contrast to the muddy-brown fur. The rest of her body was covered in well-fitted armor fabricated from the tanned hide of some type of animal.

<*This would be the perfect setup to strip us of what little security we have,*> Cain cautioned.

But Yilmaz spoke before I could. "Tactically, you're asking us to give up any defensive maneuvering we might have. And while I've indulged in my curiosity,

I'm not inclined to comply. What assurances can you give us we won't be attacked… down here?"

Risa frowned and glanced at Lunna. "This is a haven, a space we have kept from the eyes and ears of the Purified."

"But that doesn't guarantee anything for us, though, does it?" Yilmaz said.

Out of the corner of my eye, I caught the master shifting his weight as Miles's hand moved to a pocket in his uniform.

A hooded figure stepped out of the shadows, and without thinking, I activated the Vulture. "I thought you said the Eeri wouldn't follow us down here?"

"They will not," a deep voice rumbled from within the hood. A hand reached up and pulled the covering back.

The master snarled and leaped forward. "Declare!"

A very Glipglow-looking figure swung their gaze to the master then bowed with a low rumble. "Our apologies to this nest. We are known as"—there was a string of words I couldn't understand—"but you may call me Trax. We have agreed to aid Risa in stabilizing the Error."

The master didn't budge but maintained a defensive posture between us and the Broken. "No hatchling would betray their nest."

"We are not of the den mother. We are a poor imitation and are of the Broken, of level three. An early construct," Trax explained with another low rumble.

The master took a step forward then reached out and touched Trax with one of his talons.

Risa hurried to his side. "Please, no technology. If any is used—"

"Allow them this one assurance," Trax countered.

"Master?" I asked.

"They speak the truth. There are no indicators they have traveled to be seated at the tail of the den mother. They are a hatchling without a proper nest."

I glanced over at Cain, who shrugged slightly. "Yilmaz?" I asked.

"An interesting piece of information, but doesn't answer my original concerns," she said.

"We can make exceptions." Trax motioned to Lunna. "Mask the signals, but do not deactivate. This is a risk we will take."

So, you're in charge then, huh? The way Lunna and Risa didn't put up a fuss made me confident of that assessment. But even though they followed Trax's orders, they were clearly not happy. Lunna hissed each time she raised her hand and ran it over us, and she hesitated a bit when she turned to the master and they snapped at her—not in a friendly manner at all.

"The others will require standard masking signals, but I'm unsure how to mask your signature," Lunna said with a glance at Trax. "We would need to modify several dampening pins, I believe."

"Dampening pins?" Miles asked.

"Normally used for those who must work with the Purified but wish to find solace from time to time in the Below," Trax answered and gestured at Risa, who craned her neck to one side and swept back her dark hair to reveal a small silver dot behind an ear. "A risk to be sure, but for those who are required to still serve in some capacity, it is necessary."

"A risk?" I asked.

"Only for those who might be discovered by the Purified. But not for you, we assure you."

Some unknown part of what Trax said made Yilmaz step up. "Just get it over with."

She bent her head to one side, and with a quick jab, Lunna inserted the dampening pin. Miles was a touch reluctant but didn't protest, and neither did Cain. Evidently, if it was good enough for Yilmaz, it was good enough for them. And since I wasn't sporting any bioupgrades, all I had to surrender was my bracelet.

When Lunna was back in front of the master, they said, "If you would scan us again, you'll find we won't be a risk."

"We are grateful," Trax said.

"Alright, we've followed you and given in to your security measures. I think it's time for answers," I said and added with a well-timed cough, "and some help."

"Yes," Risa answered and quickly glanced at Trax. "Would you care for refreshments as well?"

I opened my mouth to protest, but Cain elbowed me. "That would be acceptable," he said.

<Really?>

<I don't like it when you're hangry.>

I gaped at him as he sniffed. *<They'd better not have zips.>*

"That is acceptable. Please, if you will follow us," Trax said.

As we shuffled off after our hosts—again—I leaned

on Cain, taking stock of where we'd landed. No doubt, we were underground, given the lights suspended along the rocky walls and ceiling. *Another cave. Great. Just great.* But this one was cheerfully bright, the lights a dazzling array of colors and flanked by colorful vendor stalls. As my nerves settled, I was shocked by how many individuals were in the Below with us.

The number was in the hundreds if my estimator was working correctly—hundreds of different levels of the Broken moved around the stalls or stood behind them, trying to sell their goods. I realized that everything I was seeing was old-school, like ancient old-school—no tech anywhere in sight, not any I could spy with my little eye, at least.

Risa and Trax led us down a side tunnel, which was a little skimpy on space for the two Glipglows. The master was grumbling behind me, but the tunnel eventually opened into another cavern. The scene was absolutely breathtaking. The rock was carved into dozens of intricate columns, archways, windows, balconies, and doorways.

Cain tugged on my arm to keep me moving as I gaped at the craftsmanship. I wondered how long they'd taken to build it. The area was a xenologist's dream come true—mysterious species and unknown customs, set before a jaw-dropping background.

Our hosts passed through one doorway, and a large table filled to the brim with steaming-hot food greeted us. And I wasn't the only one who was hungry.

"Please sit and eat. We will see to the Error," Trax said and gestured at the chairs placed around the table.

"I'm going with her," Cain insisted.

"Our apologies, but it would be safer if you did not. We maintain a clean space for medical work, and the scrubbers would have to be refitted for your biology."

"We will go," the master said.

Trax gave a little bow. "That would be acceptable."

<*I don't like it,*> Cain said.

<*The master will watch over me. You know that.*>

Reluctantly, Cain gave in.

<*It'll be alright,*> I assured him. <*Just save me some food.*>

I glanced over my shoulder and saw Miles tug at Cain, getting him to sit down. That was good. Cain needed to look after himself too. We all did, or none of us would get out of this sticky mess with the Eeri and the Star Eaters alive.

Trax escorted us through a handful of different rooms until we stopped in front of a doorway with the telltale sound of a force field running through it. "It is a scrubber field. There is nothing to be concerned with. It merely maintains a clean environment. Please follow me."

I'd expected a few medical platforms but saw a strange gelatinous substance piled up on one side of the room. Opposite that was a wall of screens.

"An integrated matrix?" the master asked, reaching out to touch the mixture with a talon.

"Yes. We spent many years studying this avenue of technology. The Purified had hopes of adapting it for healing the Shell. But the avenue of exploration proved unstable. We took what we could and have used it to help the Broken. It will be adequate for what we need today."

"Master?" I asked. "Risks I should know about?"

"This is an integrated medical matrix, developed on the Glipglow home world for emergency use onboard long-haul transports. It provides an immediate mixture of antibiotics and stimulants. Plus, the added nano-tech can assess and begin repairs faster than manually scanning and setting up the needed equipment. Its projection capabilities will provide us an accurate scan of the genetic degradation and real-time manipulation extrapolations. Far superior to what we've been able to provide so far. The matrix has been approved for interspecies use."

"And you're sure this is going to be safe?" I asked, eying the dubious-looking mound of jelly.

The master reached out and held a talon within the strange substance once more. After a few minutes, a deep thrum vibrated through the room. "We're satisfied this poses no risk."

"Alright, good enough for me," I said. "What do I do?"

"If you will allow us, we will lay you on the matrix. Please continue to breathe normally. The matrix will coat your airways but will still allow for continued breathing. A mild relaxing aid and anesthesia will also be applied. You will not feel a thing."

I glanced back at the master, who gave me a nod. "Alright. Let's do this."

The sensation was the strangest I'd felt yet, which was saying something. Together, they lifted me and gently placed me on top of the jelly. At first, I seemed to be floating, then I slowly sank. I'd thought it would be cold to the touch, but it wasn't. The jelly was warm, just the perfect temperature to help my muscles unwind. As the substance coated my chest, I tried to lift my head.

"Please relax. And breathe normally."

Easy for you to say. But I did the best I could, my strong dislike of small spaces notwithstanding. *<Cain, I need a distraction. What are you eating?>*

<They've provided a wide assortment of dishes, many of which I have no name for. There seem to be three different types of meat, an assortment of bugs, various sauteed vegetation—>

<Hold up. Did you say bugs?*>*

<Yes. There are some that are long and skinny and appear to be coated in some kind of grain. And there are a handful of ones I would describe as beetles.>

<Try one. What do they taste like?> Bugs were a great source of nutrition, but Pops had cultivated a strong dislike of the idea, so he'd never made a fuss when his kids had turned up their noses at the idea. But when I got older, I ventured on my own to a few food stalls that advertised the tasty treats. My favorite had been a tiny insect imported from Old Earth: chocolate-covered ants, crunchy and perfect for snacking.

<I… I have not had pleasurable experiences with insect-based foods in the past. I believe it has to do with my Dar ancestry.>

<Well, that's a bummer.> The gel had covered my face, and I took a tentative breath. When nothing happened but the strange sensation of something trickling down the back of my throat, I took another one—no problem breathing.

<What else?>

<There is a rather good spiced drink they've provided. Something I think you would enjoy.>

<Save some for me, alright?> Since I was fully engulfed by the jelly, I was feeling drowsy. *<I think I'm going to go to sleep for a bit.>*

<Mahia? Is everything…> But his voice trailed off as I drifted to sleep.

16

Revelations and Announcements

My dreams were a tangled mess of the events on Epo-5 and visions of the Celestial Plain. Lucas was there, laughing at me as he wound the Third around Cain, choking him, while Pops and my mom stood off to one side, holding hands and just watching me. I tried to run over and help Cain, but a Path Maker exploded out of the black sand and blocked my path. When I darted around it, Cain and Lucas were gone, and in their place was my mom, cooing and gently rocking a baby.

She caught sight of me and motioned me closer. Hesitantly, I walked up to her, but someone walked past me—Pops. He smiled and reached out to pull the blanket back, but as soon as he did, he pulled his hand back and shrank away in horror. My mom didn't take notice but continued to rock and make baby noises. Curious but feeling slightly sick to my stomach, I took a few steps closer to see what she was holding.

It was me but not me. My baby face stared up at me,

but instead of a mouth, I had a beak, and three feathers grew where I should've had a head of baby fuzz.

I screamed and stumbled backward.

A voice cut through my screams. "The patient is crashing. Administer five—"

I screamed again and stumbled backward into something hard. I turned and looked up at a Broken, its blue robe gently flapping in the wind as it walked on by. I didn't understand what I was seeing. *Is something actually in the robe? Or is it moving on its own?* No, that wasn't possible. I shook my head and rubbed my eyes. When I looked again, I saw something in the shape of a human, but its skin was so thin I could see its veins, muscles, and tendons. When it stopped and turned, I shrank back as I watched its twin hearts beating and its lungs gently rising and falling.

Then I blinked, and instead of the Broken, it was the Third, formed in its strange reflection of me. Then we were back, standing on the black beach with the waves of light gently lapping at our feet.

An electrical shock ran through my body, and I flopped on the sand like a fish.

"Another one."

A second shock ran through me, and when my eyes fluttered open, I was looking at a very distorted image of two Glipglows staring back.

"Mahia. Can you hear us?"

I grunted and tried to nod my head.

"Good. We need you to take deep, even breaths, and please reassure your heart's blood everything is fine."

I did as the master instructed. *<I'm good. I'm here.>*

<*You weren't just a few minutes ago.*> I heard the heart-break behind his words.

<*What happened?*>

<*I lost you. And they wouldn't let me through. So now Miles and Yilmaz are… Well, they stopped me.*>

<*Alright. It's okay. Everything is okay. I'm here now,*> I told Cain, but the words were as much to reassure myself as him.

"Mahia, we need you to stay in the matrix for another… twenty-three minutes. The reclamation process was further along than we suspected. The damage done to many of your internal organs is worse than first expected. You are healing, but we do not want to pull you out too soon. Extra time within the matrix will not do any harm," the master said.

I grunted again and let my eyes drift shut. *What in the worlds did I just see? Was that my imagination or something else?* As I lay there, wanting to figure it out but also shying away from the image of baby me, a thought struck me.

<*Cain? Is Risa still there? Can you ask her some questions for me?*>

<*Yes. Hold on.*>

Cain was agitated and rightly so. If he'd felt a pinch of what I'd experienced when Yilmaz captured him, I knew what he'd gone through.

<*What do you want to know?*>

<*Ask Risa… Ask her about the Broken that was constructed to contact the Star Eaters. What did they look like?*>

After a significant pause, Cain answered, <*Risa is saying that the Purified had to try several forms until they settled on one that the Star Eaters… Wait… Sorry. I wanted to make sure I understood her correctly. They tried several forms until they found one that appealed to the Star Eaters. Humanoid. No, wait, human. Specifically human. But it was modified in a variety of ways.>*

<Clear skin?>

After another pause, not as long, he said, *<Yes. How did you know?>*

<Ask her about those Broken. What happened to them? What did they do?> I was sure I knew the answer, but I wanted confirmation of what she'd resisted telling me before.

<They… Oh.>

<Cain?>

<Mahia, maybe you should hear this for yourself.>

<No. I just needed confirmation. Those Broken had offspring, the Errors that evaded the Purified. The reason why my maternal line carries Eeri DNA. I'm descended from those particular Broken.>

<I… Yes. Risa says that is correct. They hid from the Purified because they didn't want to be reclaimed. Over time, they mixed with others who were biologically compatible, in turn inspiring others to resist and…>

A wave of astonishment washed through him.

<What?>

<The war. The whole reason for the Cricade Wars.>

<Ask her what triggered it.>

That time, a long gap of silence ensued, and I was betting Miles and Yilmaz had gotten involved in the conversation as well.

<Risa says that the Purified maintain… what we would consider spies amongst the known worlds—a way to keep tabs on what is happening on other worlds. Plus, they worked to find the

Broken and the resulting Errors who have evaded reclamation. Not only that, but they were aware of what the Sun Worshipers were attempting to do and were afraid they were getting close to succeeding—to making contact with the Celestial Plain. On the outside, Kel Station was to be a trading hub, but the Eeri were going to use it as a way to reclaim the Broken and the Errors. But there was an uprising within the Broken who helped build Kel Station, and in order for the Purified to maintain their secrecy—and the fact the Star Eater cultists were of their own doing—they went to war. With every confidence they would win.>

Hubris at its finest. <Wait, I think I'm missing something. Wouldn't at least some of the species have figured out what the Eeri had done? How they made contact and have some awareness of the Broken? I mean, that's how their whole outreach program works.>

<Hang on.>

I waited for what felt like an obnoxious amount of time. *<Cain?>*

When he didn't respond, I opened my eyes. The room looked strange through the jelly, but even with it distorting my view, I didn't see either Glipglow in the room. I grunted a few times then decided I'd had enough. I wiggled around like a fish flopping on dry ground. I'm sure it was quite a comical sight, and thank goodness no one was there to witness it. But I managed to get a hand free of the jelly before the master returned.

"Hatchlings are always impatient," he muttered as he grabbed my hand and pulled.

I came free of the jelly matrix with a loud pop and landed in a sticky pile on the floor. "Where's Cain?" I asked.

"They have taken the others to... We are unsure how

to translate the name. The view port may be adequate. They instructed us to retrieve you and bring them to you."

"What's happened?" I asked. *<Cain, what's going on?>*

The master helped me up and handed me a towel to dry off with, then a fresh jumpsuit. It wasn't the best fitting one I'd ever worn, but it would do. And Cain was still silent.

"What's going on?" I asked.

"Follow me," the master rumbled. I had to jog to keep up with him as we zigzagged through rooms and corridors. *Good thing one of us can remember where to go.*

We finally stopped and entered a small room, where a large screen had been placed on the far wall. "I thought you said no tech?"

Risa glanced over at me. "This room is shielded. We can't safely operate in the blind."

That made a certain bit of sense, but I didn't have to like it. "What's going—"

"Shh." Miles waved a hand at me.

Annoyed, I stalked over to stand beside Cain.

<Why aren't you answering me?> When I turned my attention to the screen, I had my answer. The broadcast signal wasn't great, no doubt jumping through hundreds of relay stations to reach us. But it was clear enough for me to recognize Chancellor Heron. The Emperor of Old Earth was with her.

Chancellor Heron stood and spread her arms wide. "It is with a heavy heart that we must acknowledge the current political situation within the known worlds. While none of us want to revisit the ravages of war so soon after the Cricade War, we must protect the vulnerable. Our collected intelligence operatives"—she gestured at the emperor—"have provided disturbing reports coming out of the Erith system, which I'm sure many of you have already heard about through various news outlets. The emperor and I have signed an agreement to combine our collective fleets and are in negotiations with the Glipglows and Telts to join with us.

"What we have learned is that the Star Eater cult has ravaged Igridian Prime and possess a technology we have been unaware of, cannibalizing the Erith system's sun as well. All attempts at negotiation have been ignored, and we cannot allow this to continue or endanger any more lives."

The chancellor stepped back, and a new face appeared, one I didn't recognize.

<Who's that?>

<Subcommandant Hild.>

"The InterGalactic Justice system confirms these reports and has reached out to the Jumjul for aid. We are discouraged to report they have refused our request for support at this time, and upon my authority, the chancellor and the emperor have agreed to work with the agents of the InterGalactic Justice System to reach out to the Eeri. While tensions have long been high between our worlds and theirs, this is a threat that cannot be ignored by any world. We are hopeful they will agree to a joint task force, and along with whoever else may take up our cause, we will put an end to this threat."

"Fool," Yilmaz snapped and stalked out of the room.

When Miles turned to go after her, I stopped him. "No, let me."

Yilmaz hadn't gone far. "He knows better. I didn't release those records so he could make a power play," she fumed.

I kept my mouth shut, for once seeing the commandant completely out of control. And maybe I was a little too pleased about that.

"That damn fool. He's going to start a whole new war. And not over the Star Eaters, mind you"—she looked at me with disgust—"but with the Jumjul. What happened on the *Samaritan* was bad enough, but I could've talked our way out of that snag, especially given what we've learned about the Eeri. The Jumjul have no love of the Star Eater cult and have tried for years to bring them to justice as well. I had all the pieces in my hand in order to get the Eeri to work with us or else I would threaten to spill their dirty little secret."

"Blackmail, then? That's what you were going to do?" I asked.

"What other options did I have?" She looked at me and snorted. "Did you think you would be able to solve this? What level of diplomatic training or interspecies relationship communication have you had? Where are your years of having to do backdoor deals just to keep the peace? Have you sacrificed everything you hold dear just in order to—"

And just like that, her control snapped back into place, which was probably a good thing. I didn't like Yilmaz, not one bit. And I didn't care about what personal sacrifices the woman might've made. She was ruthless and heartless. Had she made any other kind of approach with me on the *Justus,* I might've been willing to tell her what was going on and to seek help from the IGJ—but not after what she did to Cain. And having her here was a constant reminder of that pain and how I'd decided to use her instead of throwing her out an airlock.

"I might not have had your fancy training, but let's not forget"—I leaned toward her—"I'm an Orion, after all."

Whatever response she was expecting from me, that certainly wasn't it. I drew back, a tad smug at the startled look on her face, and turned to leave her stewing in her own juices.

17

The Below

We replayed the message a few more times, searching for any details or hidden messages tucked away in the speeches. But aside from outlining their next steps of coordinating their respective fleets, not much else was there. But Miles had a thoughtful look on his face as we moved back to our original room with the table—miraculously—still loaded with steaming-hot food.

"Miles, care to share your thoughts with the group?" I asked as I filled my plate. *The rest of them might not be hungry, but I'm still starving.*

"Not yet."

I shrugged and speared a piece of meat. "Your chef should get together with these guys. These dishes are amazing. I haven't tasted spices like these before."

Miles nodded absentmindedly. *What had he seen on his brother's face that we didn't?* The emperor was the only one who hadn't said a word.

I turned out to be hungrier than I'd thought, and I finished my plate plus seconds and maybe a bit of thirds in record time. Leaning back and bursting to the gills,

I took a small sip of a warm tealike beverage to cleanse my palate. "So, where are we, exactly?" I asked.

Risa took a sip from her own wooden mug then gently set it down in front of herself. Both of her hands wrapped around it as steam wafted off the liquid. "We are in the Below, the sanctuary for the Broken. Once a Broken has served their purpose or has been identified as an Error, the Purified initiate the reclamation program."

"And so you've created a way to, what... free the Broken?" I asked.

She glanced at Trax, who gave Risa an encouraging nod. "In a way. We do what we can, but each one saved is a risk. They created the Broken for specific purposes and functions. It can take time to break free of that programming. And there are many who can't."

"Once they've broken free, then what?" Cain asked. "Live down here for the rest of their lives?"

Risa nodded. "Yes. Many choose to remain here. Despite our genetic appearance, this is our home world. But for others... they choose to leave, to hide amongst the known worlds or to join with other groups of Broken who live free of the Purified."

"Why would any of you choose to stay? Don't you live under the constant threat of being discovered?" I asked.

Trax nodded. "We do, but for many, it is a risk they choose to take. We do not use the translated term Purified lightly. This is the closest word we can use for how the Eeri—those truly hatched from the Shell—consider themselves. To leave this world and be present amongst other species would stain the honor between themselves and the Shell. And while many of us can break our programming, this attitude is still hard to overcome. Some of the Broken even believe that, one day, they will be able to be reborn and unite with the Shell."

"Great. More purist crap," I muttered.

"No, you misunderstand. It is hard to put into words. These are concepts the Purified do not discuss with others," Risa said. "Consider the concept more of a… religious belief. Or perhaps a philosophical one. If they had an aversion to other species, do you think they would create the Broken?"

Trax added, "It is a cosmological balance, one they do not wish to tamper with, at least not again."

"What's that supposed to mean?" Cain asked.

"Are you satisfied with the refreshments?" Trax asked, evading Cain's question.

"Answer him," Yilmaz said, being her usual bossy self.

"We will. But in order to do so, I believe it will be easier if we move to the sanctum," Trax replied. And before any of us could protest, he added, "We understand we're asking much of you, but we require your patience as we have debated the best method for providing you with the information you seek. Please, come with us."

"Well, at least I can see how these guys made it as diplomats," I said. "All polite and whatnot in their wheeling and dealing."

Cain shot me a look to quiet me.

As we followed our hosts back out into the maze of the Below, I glanced over at Cain. *<Any thoughts about what your mom said?>*

<No. She's taken hold of an opportunity to bring the Aligned Worlds closer to Old Earth, something she's wanted to do for

years.> Something lay behind his words, a bit of disgust and guilt.

<Are you thinking about what happened with your father and Elea? Do you think if your mother knew what really happened, that it would change things?>

<No. My mother loved my father, but in her own way. She's a politician and one who had to play on the outside for quite some time before gaining traction. She wouldn't let this chance slip by, no matter the past.>

I made sure to not broadcast my next thought because the way he was describing his mother reminded me of Yilmaz. Both were willing to do whatever they thought necessary and cross lines I didn't agree with. But I wasn't in their shoes, either. I didn't have the responsibility of overseeing the lives of billions. *Or do I? Aren't I responsible for the lives lost on Igridian Prime? And wherever else the Star Eaters might go if we can't stop them in time?*

I'd thought I got through to the Third on Epo-5, helping them to reconnect with the Star Eaters and to stop consuming biological life in order to fuel the Path Makers. But I'd been wrong—perhaps a miscommunication because we didn't have enough information to fully understand who exactly they were. Or maybe they were so completely different in their way of life and thinking that we couldn't make them understand the destruction they were causing. Even if their motivations were simply to survive and go home, they were still destroying life.

But what right do I or anyone else have to tell them to stop? Can we push our cultural expectations or ethical views on a species that's entirely different? Or should we try to understand and figure out a way to work together?

Those were uncomfortable thoughts I didn't want to dwell on, at least at the moment. But I knew I was going to have to find answers to them sooner rather than later.

As our hosts took us back through the main cavern, I glanced at the ground. I nudged Cain and tapped Miles on the shoulder. "Look." I pointed at the floor. I'd been so mesmerized with the grand buildings the first time we came through that I hadn't noted what we were walking on. Carved into the rock was an impressive and mindboggling display of craftsmanship, an intricate map of the galaxy and its known worlds.

We stopped and admired the work. Miles studied it for a few minutes then moved to crouch next to one of the carved planets.

"Old Earth," he whispered and ran a hand over the intricate outlines of the continents. "It's been a long time. Too long."

He didn't have to say anything else. I knew he had to be thinking about his brother and the tangled mess the emperor was getting Old Earth sucked into.

I turned away, giving him a moment of privacy, and touched Cain's arm. "Where is the world your father liked to visit? What was it called?"

"It was—" Cain started.

"We ask for your understanding, but we must keep moving on," Trax interrupted quietly but firmly. "While we have remained hidden from the Purified for centuries, your arrival and that of the Jumjul jeopardize us. We cannot afford to waste valuable time."

Miles stood and brushed himself off. "Of course."

Trax had mentioned taking us to a sanctum, but what I saw wasn't what I'd pictured. We'd been led to an art gallery. Someone had lovingly hung beautiful representations of art from across the known worlds on the walls with soft lights perched above them. Miles's face lit up like a kid in a candy store. Even Yilmaz looked taken aback. Trax gave us a few moments to wander through the gallery before giving a polite cough and drawing our attention to one piece covered by a soft white cloth. The fabric sparkled under the lights.

"We have collected the stories of the Broken who have gone before us and those who have found freedom from the Purified. All the Broken who live in the Below take an oath, standing here, under the gaze of our true history. We have longed for many generations to be able to complete this illuminating piece of art, but we are pleased to be able to share at least this much with you." Trax pulled back the cloth to reveal a section of the *Three Heralds*.

"You've got to be kidding me," Miles said, along with a few more colorful exclamations. He stepped up close, carefully examining the piece before looking at Trax. "I have one section and have been searching for the others for years. If only I'd known…"

I glanced at Yilmaz, who was remaining quiet. "So does she," I said, pointing at the commandant when she didn't speak up.

"What?" Miles exclaimed and whirled around to face her. "You? Of all people, you have a piece?"

"I appreciate art," Yilmaz said with a shrug.

"And all this time, you weren't going to tell me, were you? Just hide the fact you already had a piece," he snapped.

"Why should I? That information had no bearing on our arrangement," Yilmaz said with a shrug.

"What arrangement?" Cain asked.

"On Epo-5, when I gave up one of my most prized possessions in order to save you," Miles grumbled.

I stared at him. "You were going to give her your piece of the *Three Heralds*?" How Miles seemed to treasure his little—or, rather, not so little—collection of items made me realize we meant far more to him than I could've imagined. "Wow. Um, thank you."

"Desperate times, and all that," he said.

But he wasn't going to let Yilmaz off scot-free. They started bickering—more like a one-sided gripe fest as the would-be emperor grilled her over the details of the section she owned—and I inspected the artwork.

This piece was no less exquisite than the one Miles had displayed. The fifteenth cycle of art for the Tahhs was in full force on this section as well, but upon a closer look, the way the tiny mosaic pieces were placed didn't appear to be Cresta Lop Tahh's work. But that wasn't out of line with what I knew. On a piece of this size, artists might employ students or even other well-known artists to help complete a piece, especially if a deadline had to be met.

Miles's piece had featured a capsa tree, which the Star Eaters on Epo-5 had claimed was actually a Ray of Reverence, a gift *to* the One, from which sprang the

Two. And this piece also depicted a capsa tree, one that looked eerily familiar.

"What was it that they've speculated?" I asked. "That the capsa tree wasn't native to Pola Tahh but possibly genetically engineered?"

"Yes. That they know the tree isn't native to Pola Tahh. The idea of genetic engineering has been considered." He slowly turned around. "Which seems to be a theme with the Eeri."

"You are both very observant," Trax commented.

"But the myths discuss the tree as a gift from the One," Miles said.

"A blurring of truth through time. Quite common on all worlds. History is never perfectly preserved," Risa said. "What they call the capsa tree is, in fact, an offshoot of the Talon's Nest, the once-dominant tree species on this world, a sacred part of the Shell."

"And so that's why this is so important to you?" Cain asked Trax.

"It is a piece of truth, hidden and left for us to preserve—a reminder of the past and a way to inspire and guard for our future."

I turned and stared at Trax then Risa. "Meaning that this must be a point in time when the Eeri weren't so secretive, or else why give away something they consider sacred? And this must also have been where the Eeri bumped into the Celestial Plain. So tell me—what's the truth here? What kind of connection could you have with Pola Tahh?"

"The Sundering."

18

History Lessons

"When the Shell was young and full of life, there were no Broken, and the Purified were ready to look beyond their world. Pola Tahh was rich in mineral mining, so the Purified reached out, eager to begin a trading relationship.

"Initial inquiries went well, and a relationship was formed. After some time, the Purified became comfortable with this partnership, and a part of the Shell was transported to Pola Tahh, allowing the Purified to live and work on that world.

"But those of the Celestial Plain had also arrived. Curious to a fault, the Pola Tahh worked hard on trying to establish communication with what they came to call the One. The Purified offered their help, but for reasons lost to us, the Pola Tahh rejected those offers. And in time, the Purified grew suspicious—jealous, even—because they perceived the One as… something sacred. When the One, from which sprang the Two, appeared to gift Pola Tahh with great power and knowledge and ignored the beauty of the Shell, the Purified became furious at this perceived insult," Trax explained.

"I think I'm getting a headache," Miles muttered.

I agreed. "Yilmaz, what does your piece of the *Three Heralds* look like? I was a little out of it at that moment, if you recall."

Yilmaz scowled and shifted her weight, a rare sign of agitation from the normally composed commandant.

"It's show and tell time. You wanted our help to stop what's happening, so get to it," I snapped.

With a resigned sigh, she said, "There's a grand cathedral-like building being constructed. One side of it has been fully rendered, while the others are open and show the interior support network."

"And that's all?" I asked.

She nodded. "Yes. Besides flourishes of vegetation."

I turned back and studied the piece hanging in front of us. "Alright, my art aficionados, correct me if I'm wrong here. But considering all three pieces, I'm assuming Yilmaz's third would have been on the… right, with Miles's in the middle and this piece on the left."

Miles joined me and leaned as close as he dared. "I would hazard a guess you're correct. See these seemingly darker pieces here?" He pointed at the right edge of the canvas. "I bet you these are a part of the capsa tree on my piece, the edges of the branches. And judging from the direction the Pola Tahh are facing here, I'm guessing they were gazing out toward that cathedral. But what's this?" His finger moved across to the far-left edge and an image of something broken, half buried in the purple-hued grass.

I took a step closer. "I thought you said the Shell wasn't allowed to be a part of all this. Did the Purified actually create the *Three Heralds*? As a way of expressing their feelings of betrayal?"

"No," Trax replied.

"Then why does this look like an egg that's been cracked—" I stopped. *Quit being so damned literal.* "Holy hell. It's a Path Maker."

Everyone jockeyed for a view of what I was seeing and eventually settled down.

"Remember what we found on Dar? What we thought was a ship?" I turned toward Cain. "I bet you anything that was a part of a Path Maker. It must've been severely damaged when it crashed on Dar and unable to fully re-form into its normal shape. And so it improvised," I said, my excitement building as the pieces came together. "They can shift into a shape they need, but their inert form, or preferred form, must be a ball or, rather, what might be perceived as a shell. Which would explain the Eeri's idea there was something shared, something sacred about them." I paused for a moment. "After what I've experienced with the Third, when they traveled to our galaxy, something went horribly wrong, and the Third and the Star Eaters couldn't work together like we thought."

"As in, how the Third was eating people?" Miles clarified.

I nodded. "Exactly. The Third's survival instinct kicked in, their need to complete their job, and when they were separated from the Star Eaters and couldn't consume the light, they turned to biological life, any life-form they could consume. This energy, whether from the sun or biological life, was the fuel for the Path Makers."

"Alright," Cain said as he ran a hand through his hair. "But then what about Pola Tahh? Where's the Third? Why didn't it consume the life there?"

I turned back to the painting. "Good question. I was so caught up in the Third's plea for help and what they were showing me that I didn't think about what had initially happened to the Star Eaters. Pola Tahh must've been the world the Star Eaters landed on… or traveled to. However that worked."

"And so the One"—Miles reached out, one finger hovering over the canvas—"is actually the Path Maker. And if we're considering it a ship, that would explain the phrase 'from which spring the Two.' It's referring to the two Star Eaters."

"Yes," I almost squealed. "Which is why the Star Eaters must've identified themselves to me that way on Epo-5, calling themselves the Two. That's not what they consider themselves but what was used to identify them on Pola Tahh, and it must've stuck."

"And the Eeri?" Cain asked.

I frowned and glanced at Trax to fill in the gaps.

But Risa was the one to speak up. "The Purified grew jealous of this relationship, of the knowledge and power they felt was gifted to the Pola Tahh and not to the Shell. But try as they might, Pola Tahh refused this area of their world to the Purified. Outraged and hurt, the Purified withdrew, vowing to never again share their knowledge so freely. It was then that the idea of the Broken was created."

"Spies," I whispered.

"Yes, to put it bluntly. The first Broken were sent back to Pola Tahh in an effort to gain access to what the Purified had been denied. And in time, they did. The Broken brought the Two from Pola Tahh here, to the heart of the Shell.

"The Purified taught the Two their language and provided them with the Woven Cloak of Ahulet as a sign of their worthiness to be a part of the Shell. But this process was arduous, and many Broken were created and destroyed during this time. But this did two things for the Shell. First, the Purified realized the Two were looking for something. And second, it allowed the Purified to perfect their work in creating the Broken.

"And so the Purified sent scores of Broken throughout the galaxy, integrating them with all levels of civilizations, to scout for potential trading partners and to try to discover what the Two desperately wanted."

"I'm assuming they did, right? They found the Third," I said.

"Yes. In time. And through another long process, the Purified found a biological species that appeared to be able to work with not only the Two but also with what you call the Third. But the Purified were cautious and have long memories. The perceived slight from dealings with the Pola Tahh have clouded their actions ever since. They didn't share this information with the Two, despite the Two freely sharing information of their own by that point, the secret to harnessing the power of the suns."

Miles let out a long, low whistle. "All this time, the Eeri had what everyone had been scrambling for and fighting over."

"But why not use it? If they'd really wanted to win the war…" Cain said.

Risa shared an uncomfortable look with Trax. "The Purified did… once."

"Once they unraveled what the Two were capable of, they crafted a technological version of what the Two were able to do with their biological version.

"While they could harness a massive amount of energy from the sun they harvested, they truly didn't understand what they were doing. They were motivated by jealousy as the Purified assumed this was the information provided to Pola Tahh.

"And it was this arrogance and pride that caused the war to break out between the Shell and the Pola Tahh. The Purified used this new technology against their former partners and did considerable damage to what the Pola Tahh held sacred, their twin suns. In retaliation, the Pola Tahh decimated the Shell," Trax clarified.

"The Sundering," Cain murmured.

"Yes," both Trax and Risa said.

"And so because of this perceived slight, the Purified have had it out for the Celestial Plain ever since?" I asked. "Or is it more that they simply don't want anyone else to have access to that kind of power?"

"Both," Trax confirmed. "And since then, the Purified have remained on the Shell, refusing to leave and vowing to destroy the Two."

"But it wasn't the Pola Tahh who suffered because of

the Eeri's arrogance," Yilmaz added unexpectedly. "It was the Lesser Seeds of Irolo. The war had far-reaching effects. During a heated battle, the fighting spilled over into a nearby system, where it was believed the Pola Tahh had a secret base. The Seed of Karth was destroyed, along with its moons. Despite the Lesser Seeds already being a spacefaring culture, the destruction resulted in billions of lives lost and generations of knowledge."

"So the Gatekeepers didn't go to the Eeri because they were allies. They came to them because they knew what the Eeri had done, what had really happened," I said. "Has it been all about revenge this entire time? Some kind of ancient hatred passed down through the generations?"

Yilmaz looked like she wanted to say something, but she pursed her lips and spun around, stalking out of the room. *Well, fine then.*

"Got any chairs in here?" Miles half joked. When Trax shook their head, Miles plopped down on the floor. "That's one full cargo load of information to absorb."

That it was. But everything was beginning to make sense—why the Eeri had begun the war and why they'd provided Pops with a way to kill all those people on the *Rapscallion. Except…* "Wait, Risa, earlier you said that my pops had betrayed the Purified. Was it because he let his children live?"

Risa hesitated, and I was prepared to stand my ground and demand answers, but a shriek of rage filled the air. As I cringed, Cain and the master rushed out the entrance of the little art gallery. After another cry of fury, Cain ducked back inside.

"That's not possible," Risa said with a stricken look at Trax. "How could they have breached the Below?"

The Glipglow's lower jaws snapped open and shut, and they stretched to their full height. "A question saved for later. Emergency procedures must be activated."

"But if we do that, then—"

"Risa, doing so far outweighs anything we might lose. We have prepared for such an event. You know this."

Risa nodded with a clenched jaw, and I had a flash of another memory. But this wasn't the time. I shook my head, trying to clear my mind. "What do we do?"

"Stay here," Trax ordered. The Glipglow charged out of the room.

Risa held up a hand as I opened my mouth. "Wait," she hissed.

"For what? If the—"

A booming voice echoed throughout the room. "The time of reclamation is at hand. Fight and claim your status among the halls of our brethren."

"There will be a moment of pain, but we would advise you pull out your dampening pins. You will need your technology to survive what's coming," Risa told us.

"No offense, but we didn't come here to get caught up in your war against the Purified. We have our own battles to face," Miles said as he yanked out his dampening pin.

"And I thought you told us the Purified wouldn't follow us here," Cain said as he, too, winced.

"And they shouldn't have. I don't know what went wrong, but come, we must hurry." Risa tried to usher us out of the room.

"We need a way out of here," I said, ignoring her and turning toward the others.

"Agreed. We can navigate our way back to where we started," the master said. "But it may take some time to analyze and hack into their transportation tech."

"There's no need for that," Risa huffed. "Come with me."

"I'm sorry, but it's like Miles said. We didn't come here to fight in another—"

"We're not asking that of you. We understand what you came here to do and that you must live. I will show you a way out."

<Do we believe her?>

<I don't think we've got the option not to,> Cain replied.

"Miles? Master?"

They both nodded in silent agreement.

"Then lead on," I said.

We hurried after Risa, squeezing through even narrower corridors than what we'd already experienced. I half feared the master would get stuck. But we soon ran into Lunna and a handful of others outfitted in the same armor.

"Report," Risa ordered.

"The Purified have breached the northern entrance, and the pods in that section have been discovered. We've begun sending the Broken to the southern and western pods. Kiskian and her group have engaged the Purified and are currently holding position. But I fear for not much longer." Lunna looked at us. "Will they fight?"

"If they fight, they will die. And if Mahia and her

people die, then the known worlds will perish as well," Risa said.

"And yet the Purified have breached the Below because of the Error. But they will not stand and defend us?" Lunna snapped.

"You would have them die? Here? And what of the sacred trusts we carry? Of the oaths we've all sworn? Would you forsake those as well?"

Lunna's eyes blazed with anger, but she didn't argue.

"Wait, where is Yilmaz?" I asked, realizing the commandant hadn't joined back up with us. I'd assumed she'd simply slipped out of the room for a few moments to herself. *Should have seen that coming.*

"Damn that slippery eel," Miles muttered. "But I think that answers how your defenses were breached. But we don't have time to go after her. I don't know about you, but I could use a good cardio workout at this point."

"And you think we'd stand a chance against the Eeri? There isn't any tech down here. Their weapons are old-school, and I can bet you that the Eeri aren't going to play fair," Cain replied.

"No. You will not fight. I will get you to the pods. They have been prepared for emergencies when a Broken must be transported past Purified eyes. We'll head for the eastern section. But if the Purified have broken through in the north, it won't take them long to find the eastern enclosures. The way isn't as convoluted as it is here."

"Then we're agreed," Cain said. "Show us."

I turned to Lunna, unable to ignore the twinge of guilt in my chest. "I know you don't want to hear it, but I'm grateful for this—for your help and what we've learned here. And I wish you luck."

Lunna glared but replied in a stiff voice, "You are now of the Broken. May your Shell be strong and the air beneath you keep you steady and true."

We raced through the underground sanctuary, the sound of fighting growing stronger all around us. I desperately wanted to help. Risa and Trax had taken me in without hesitation. By helping me, I'd brought this on them. *The Orion family strikes again,* I thought ruefully as we rounded another corner. But I didn't know what I could do. If we died there—and I knew the Eeri would kill us if they found us—then nobody knew what would become of the billions of lives in jeopardy across the known worlds.

When we reached the pods, a small cluster of Broken were scrambling for places on the escape transports.

Risa started shouting, pushing them out of the way. "Come on!" she yelled.

Miles and the master elbowed their way through the small group, Miles intently listening to Risa's instructions on the pod controls.

"Cain, this isn't right," I said, grabbing his arm and dragging him away. "We can't take these pods, not when there are so many who need them instead."

"And if we don't go?" he asked.

I looked over at the Broken. "We find another way."

Cain reached out and held my arms, his eyes an intense mixture of amber and black. "The Eeri will destroy you."

"I know."

He didn't argue even though I sensed he wanted to. But he knew well enough that I wasn't going to take no for an answer. He pushed his way through the group and had a quiet word with Miles and the master. I saw nods all around and breathed a sigh of relief. Why they continued to go along with my outlandish, half-brained ideas was beyond me, but I was grateful.

The master made his way to my side. "Your courage is to be admired. They would highly celebrate a hatchling of such bravery on our world. To sacrifice yourself for the survival of the nest…" The words were unexpected and appreciated.

I sniffed, trying to hold back the sudden urge to cry. "Thank you. Your support through all of this has meant so—"

He shifted his weight and gently grabbed my hand, pulling my arm and turning it so my palm was facing up. "But it is the job of the elders to protect the hatchlings," the master said quietly. With one of his talons, he touched my skin where the HalfLife biochip had been implanted.

I had an instant to be confused, then everything went dark.

19

Double-crossing Scuttle Fish

"I don't like this," someone growled. "Our window of opportunity is rapidly closing. Risa, I thought you said they equipped these pods with shielding tech?"

"They are. But I can't guarantee it will be strong enough to let us slip by the Jumjul patrols."

"All we have to do is hold out long enough for the Glipglow cruisers to get here, right?"

I heard a low rumble of agitation followed by "Yes. Our calculations show they should arrive in the system at any moment. But there are several things which may have held—"

"Yes, yes… we know. But this is our one shot."

<Mahia?>

<You piece of space trash. I know what you did.> I blinked and tried to get my bearings.

<And I would do it again. Your actions were noble but fool-hardy. The Eeri would've destroyed you if we'd stayed.>

<Just as they'll destroy all the Broken left behind, ones who

could have used this pod to get free. I could've been a bargaining chip or blackmailed them… or anything but this!>

The pod was tiny, even worse than the shuttle we'd taken to get to Epo-5. And while Cain tried to reason with me, I ignored him. What with the cramped quarters, the only upswing was the recessed areas we were tucked up in. The pod held six little nooks, evenly spaced around its perimeter. Across from me was Cain, whom I avoided looking at, and next to him were Miles and Risa. So the master must've been tucked up in one of the areas next to me, but without leaning forward and poking my head out, I couldn't tell which side.

Above me appeared to be a series of controls, but I couldn't make head or tails of what they might be for. As tempted as I was to start randomly pushing buttons, I didn't want to accidentally blow us up.

"We've got a Jumjul vessel on approach. Let's hope the shielding holds," Miles said.

Risa reached up and double-checked. "I've pushed as much power as I can without compromising life support or navigation."

"Hold steady," Miles said. "Hold…"

"The Jumjul have moved past us," Risa reported. "We can switch over to the engines, push them a bit."

"No," Cain said. "The Jumjul might detect that. Better to stay where we are and wait. Right now, we're nothing to them. Let's not change that."

"Wait for what?" I asked, pointedly looking at Miles.

He gave me a sheepish look. "The Glipglow. Remember the master's homing signal?"

"That's your big gamble?"

"It was better than staying put and watching you die," Cain snapped. "Even if we are spotted by the Jumjul, we'll surrender, plead our case to the High Court. They don't want to see any more worlds destroyed than we do. We will just have to—"

"We? You mean me, right?" I said.

"Us," Risa corrected. "Together. You and me."

That shut me up—Cain too.

"I didn't come with you because of the affection I remember your mother feeling for you. I came because of my vows to the Broken. We've been waiting for an opportunity to tell the worlds what the Purified have done, what they've kept hidden all these years. But the risk has always been too great. Too many of our brothers and sisters still served the Purified. But now… now that the Purified have broken the sanctity of the Shell, we shall rise and tell our truth."

The speech was rousing but also jarring. I hadn't expected Risa to feel any affection toward me, not until she said it out loud. Physically, my mom was sitting across from me, but she wasn't my mom, a distinction I had to keep straight.

"We've got another Jumjul vessel, fast approaching," Miles said. "I've got a bad feeling about this one. They're boosting power, if I'm reading this correctly."

"Hold steady," Cain added. "Just like the last one. Risa?"

"All systems are still good to go," she confirmed.

I glanced up at my set of controls. Images were scrolling across a small screen along with written notations I didn't recognize. *Must be able to make them out because of their bioupgrades.* Not for the first time, I wondered if I should invest in some of those, especially if my life continued along this crazy path.

"Passing by and… clear," Miles reported. "I'm not sure what they're up to, but I'd say—"

"This is Commandant Yilmaz of the InterGalactic Justice System. Power down and prepare to be brought to justice."

"What the hell?" Miles said as he jumped.

"That dirty little double-crosser," I muttered. "I bet she had some emergency beacon this whole time and was just waiting to strike."

"Which explains how the Purified were alerted to the Below," Risa added.

"I suppose we can't outrun them in this thing, can we?"

"No," Cain said. "We've got nothing. Master?"

"No signal as of yet," the master rumbled. "But we will update the beacon."

The pod was jostled for a split second as the Jumjul locked on and dragged us into one of their cargo bays. *<I'm still upset at you. But we need a plan.>*

"We hold out for the Glipglow to arrive," Cain said. "Most likely, we'll be taken to a detention center and have to wait for processing. Maybe that'll buy us enough time."

"Sure, but time for what?" I asked, having missed part of an earlier conversation.

"You are a part of my den and, as such, will be treated accordingly under the agreements between our den mother and the High Court," the master stated.

I turned and looked at Cain, who had a rather smug

look on his face. *<If you'd been listening instead of ignoring, you would've heard me try to tell you what the master told us. But if you didn't go for it, we didn't have time to debate. This is a better option than trying to use you as blackmail or whatever half-crazed scheme you would've come up with.>*

<You're not helping yourself, buddy.>

The pod trembled then, after a loud thud, remained still. With a groan, the door was pried open, and standing squarely in the middle of a squadron of Jumjul was none other than the little scuttle fish herself.

"You will surrender all weapons, and any bioupgrades will be temporarily shut down," Yilmaz said. "Per the standard agreements between the InterGalactic Justice System and the Jumjul High Court, you will be detained aboard this vessel until your trial can be processed. You are entitled to legal representation. If you do not have any, a Jumjul advocate will be assigned to your case."

Oh, how I wanted to spit in her face. But the Jumjul marched into the pod and quickly secured each one of us.

As they escorted us out, Yilmaz continued yapping. "The charges that stand against you are listed as the following: kidnapping and illegally detaining the Commandant of the InterGalactic Justice System; kidnapping and illegally transporting the Commandant of the InterGalactic Justice System; willfully disobeying Jumjul command and fleeing from lawful detention; committing an act of sabotage against a Jumjul vessel."

"Kidnapping?" I said. "You weren't kidnapped, you little—"

<Shut it. She's baiting us.>

"I don't give a fudge nugget dipped in nuts whether

she is or not. Yilmaz is lying to you," I said, trying to acknowledge the authoritative-looking Jumjul standing beside her. "She came with us. She was helping us."

"The commandant has explained the situation. In detail," the Jumjul replied. "You will be detained and charged accordingly."

"Yilmaz! You asked for our help. You told us to—"

<Will you be quiet?>

"Mahia, for the love of Pluto, shut your mouth," Miles snapped at the same time Cain did.

But I was furious, not only at Yilmaz, but at myself. I'd fallen for her little trap. She'd done just enough to make it seem that she really was on our side, that she was going to help us. But all along, she'd just been waiting for her opportunity to double-cross us.

I struggled against my Jumjul, but it was a strong sucker and just tightened its grip with each little twist I made. They forced us to walk, and I was seeing red. *Who cares about the vast kaleidoscope of colors being broadcast throughout the Jumjul ship?* I didn't. All I cared about was getting my hands around Yilmaz's neck and—

<Snap out of it, and calm down. We're alive. We move on from here.>

"You snap out of it," I hissed and tried to glare at Cain, but his Jumjul captor shoved him, moving him ahead of me.

"As much as I admire your spunky spirit, now isn't the time," Miles said. "Hey, careful there… but seriously, Mahia dear, now is the time to channel your inner Orion—cool and collected. Use that clever little brain of yours."

<Miles is right. We don't say anything unless directly asked a question. And even then, keep it short and to the point. No openings for further questions. We don't know what Yilmaz told them or what deals she might've made with them.>

<Yes, sir.>

<This isn't a time for levity. This is serious. Without top-notch legal representation—and ones well-versed in Jumjul law—we don't stand a chance. No matter what information you think you might have, which they would listen to. Understand?>

Oh, I understood. And my anger was rapidly fading… at least toward Cain. All he was doing was trying to protect me. I just didn't like the fact that he hadn't at least told me all this first. Sure, I probably would've protested and argued for something different. *But still…*

Back to the Jumjul legal system—it was as formidable as their military. And while I might begrudgingly admit Cain was right to get us off the Eeri home world, he was wrong about this.

<But we do have top-notch legal representation.>

"I need to talk to whoever is in charge," I said.

*<Mahia! I told you—>*Agitation and a healthy dose of fear burst behind his words, and as he twisted around to look at me, a fair amount of emerald appeared in his eyes.

"The accused will remain silent," the nearest Jumjul replied.

"We were told we were entitled to legal representation. How's that going to happen if we can't talk?"

I would've sworn Cain was going to have a heart attack, judging by the look on his face and the not-so-kind words he was yelling at me.

"The accused will remain silent voluntarily or will be artificially silenced."

"Yeah, I get all that. You don't like to be pestered and whatnot. But my lawyers aren't going to be happy once they find out I've been illegally held without representation."

Apparently, the Jumjul really hated to be pestered. It must have been on their top-five list of things that really got under their skin. The Jumjul let go and zapped me. Electricity raced through my body, and my muscles seized. Unable to maintain my balance, I crashed into the Jumjul holding Cain. We were pretty lucky my stupid little stunt didn't cause us to brush up against the poisonous glands in their palms.

When I found I could at least use my mouth again, I stuttered out the name of my lawyers. "Bloodhearst and Strobe… won't be pleased… legal fees…"

The Jumjul standing over me with a decidedly unhappy gleam in their eye froze. "The accused will repeat what they just said."

I popped my jaw back and forth a couple of times. "Bloodhearst and Strobe. They're my lawyers."

The Jumjul exchanged a flurry of hand gestures until one of them reached down—with gloved hands, thank goodness—and helped me to my feet. "The austere offices of Bloodhearst and Strobe will be contacted immediately. Do they also represent the other accused?"

"You bet your shiny rockets they do," I said without a thought. I was paying a hefty amount of credits to keep those guys on retainer and had no doubt I could wiggle my way into adding the others onto my policies.

Pops might have been many things, but low on credits hadn't been one of them. Jupiter's moons, I could've paid to have Miles and half the crew of the *Samaritan* be represented.

"And I'm sure they would be pleased to hear about the excellent and compassionate treatment their clients have been given by the Jumjul," I hastily added.

<*Pushing...*>

<*What? It can't hurt, seeing how they reacted to the name.*>

After another pause, with another set of animated hand gestures, the Jumjul said, "Please, follow us, if the accused will promise to remain in Jumjul custody."

I shrugged. "Sure, why not?" And I couldn't help but shoot Cain a rather triumphant grin.

Our restraints were removed, and in no time, we were shown to a rather comfortably set up room, at least by Jumjul standards.

20

Dreaded Political Intrigue

"I will reimburse you the credits," Miles said as the door slid closed.

"No worries. I've got plenty to spare," I replied.

He quirked an eyebrow at me but didn't say anything else. Cain, on the other hand, had plenty to say. He grabbed my arm and pulled me off to the side.

"That was stupid," he started off. "Foolhardy and unnecessary." Then he pulled me in for the tightest hug I'd ever received.

<Right back at you,> I sent him. *<Did you really have to knock me out? I mean, come on.>*

<There wasn't time, and I didn't know how you'd react. The master offered, and I said yes.>

<Shifting blame there, I see,> I replied with a lighter tone. *<I'm sorry I reacted so poorly. It's just that it was a bit of a shock, and given the circumstances...>*

<I understand, but—> He pulled back and looked me square in the eye. "I won't ever promise not to do it again. I'll do whatever it takes to keep you safe."

Nobody could argue with that.

"Right back at you," I said.

"So, now what?" Miles asked as he made a quick circuit around the room.

"We wait," I said. "Given their reaction, I'm guessing they're already contacting my lawyers. Master, what about the Glipglows? What will they do when they arrive? I'm sorry to say, but I'm sure they've included you in the charges that piece of waste fuel rattled off."

"They will request our transfer and those of my den. The Jumjul have historically honored such requests from our species. We have no doubt they will do the same in this case."

"And then what?" Miles continued to push. "We're still going to be expected to stand trial, which could be tomorrow or a year from now. The Jumjul love their paperwork, but with what's been going on, they might expedite this whole affair."

"Not to mention whatever is going on with Yilmaz—" I started, but the door opened. "Well, speak of the devil."

"That is an archaic expression," she said as she stepped into the room, "but I do what I must." At some point, she'd changed back into the highly starched uniform of the IGJ. Her hair had been pulled back into a severe bun, and she looked exhausted.

"How'd you manage your little escape?" Miles casually asked.

"I don't ever go anywhere without a backup plan. And I would've expected more from someone like you," Yilmaz said.

"You made a deal with them, didn't you?" I said,

abruptly realizing what must've happened. "When they originally boarded the *Samaritan* or somehow when you sent the message—something that we missed."

"Very good. The Jumjul and I were curious as to what the Eeri would present to you. There have been suspicions for ages over their involvement with the Star Eaters, but nothing that could be proved. I simply needed the last of the information you so helpfully supplied."

I crossed my arms and studied the woman as Miles peppered her with questions. Something was off, but I couldn't put my finger on it. When we'd been in the Hall of the Broken, I would've bet my life on her sincerity, wanting us to do whatever was needed in order to stop the Star Eaters. I couldn't stand her, but she had been honest then—I was sure of it—if maybe for the only time in her life. *But now? Now is different.* Wrinkles of concern creased her forehead, and she held the corners of her mouth a bit too tightly. I wasn't an expert at body language by any means, but even I could spot how nervous she was.

<Cain? What's up with her?>

<I don't know, but I see it too. Perhaps she's made one deal too many.>

That could've been. She seemed to have been playing fast and loose with deals during the past few months. *And there's always that pesky notion of factions within factions within factions.*

"What's your plan for dealing with the Star Eaters?" I asked. *Why beat around the bush now?*

She blinked. "We will stop them."

"How?"

"That remains to be seen," she said.

<She's lying.>

<How do you know?> Cain asked.

<I'm not sure, but my gut is telling me something is wrong.>

"So, you've won then. Gotten what you wanted all along. To stop me."

"It would appear so," she said.

"Appear so?" I asked. "I don't think there's anything questionable about our situation. We're prisoners. Of the Jumjul. The one government powerful enough in the known worlds to make sure—"

Yilmaz stiffened and looked away.

"Cain, do you remember when we were on Lunar 5 and we were discussing Jorge and Project Clear Sight?"

He shrugged. "Yes."

"You asked me if I'd been keeping up with the current political situation or following along on the whisper nets," I said.

"I remember our conversations, but not necessarily all the details. I can't say that what happened afterward did my memory any favors," he said with a rather nasty snarl directed at Yilmaz.

"I distinctly remember you made a comment about rumors of governments considering negotiations with the Eeri, in return for pushing back against the Jumjul."

"The rumors are true," Miles added. "My dear brother, for one—or, rather, the insipid council members he keeps close at hand. He's never liked feeling like a second fiddle, and humanity isn't the big, bad species to look out for, no matter how they've tried to emulate the Jumjul or piggyback off other species' work."

"And when we watched the feed of Chancellor Heron and the IGJ, one person present remained quiet," I added. "The emperor." I turned to look at Miles. "Factions within factions, right?"

He gave me a rather brilliant grin. "Right."

I stepped closer to Yilmaz and lowered my voice. "Let's get this straight. I don't like you. In fact, I think I may hate you. But if there's one thing I firmly believe about you, it's that you want to stop the Star Eaters. But you're in a sticky little web of intricate backdoor deals and half-truths. Am I right?"

She nodded.

"For all your bluster, you've been walking on the edge of the abyss. And thanks to Lucas and what he did, he put the known worlds on edge, making an already precarious political climate even more dangerous, not to mention what the Jumjul might do if they found out the weapon Lucas stole had been developed by the IGJ."

Fury flashed in her eyes.

"Aw, and there's the sore spot. What would happen if they figured that out? What would they do to you? And there's no way you want the Eeri in charge, either. Because of your status as a Gatekeeper, you know what they've done, and—deny it all you want—there's a bit of personal revenge in there, isn't there? So you've got to make sure the Jumjul don't know how deeply you're involved in all of this, to maintain your grip as the Commandant of the IGJ, and to maneuver the pieces on the board to make sure the deals with the Eeri can't go through. Which means playing it up to the Jumjul, no matter the cost, right?"

I hated political intrigue—too messy and populated with dishonest individuals who always seemed to silence the few honest ones.

"This entire mess could've been avoided if you'd just been up-front with me from the beginning," I hissed. "But you were worried, and the pressure was mounting. So you got sloppy, thought you could intimidate me on the *Justus*."

"I can't step down as commandant. Do you realize the chaos that would result if that were to happen?" she asked.

"Chaos? I think you're valuing yourself a tad bit too much." I scoffed.

"Really? Do you think so? Years of carefully crafting allegiances and loyalty, working to maintain the peace between species who would sooner rip each other apart than sit down and negotiate. Years of doing all the dirty work required to maintain a semblance of justice on the known worlds. The sacrifices I've made—the agents I've ordered to do whatever was necessary. Then *he* gets up there and parades around as if he knows what he's doing. If he alienates the Jumjul, we'll be fighting a war we can't win on two fronts—the Star Eaters and the military might of the Jumjul. No world can afford that."

"Not to mention the fact the Jumjul will help you stay in power," Cain said.

With a dramatic sigh, Miles added, "Which would explain my brother's silence on the broadcast. Rare of him to miss an opportunity to speak and try to proclaim the might of Old Earth. But by staying silent, he let the IGJ do all the talking for him. Easy to play the victim then, if everything goes south and he doesn't get his way of seeing the Jumjul taken down a peg or two."

"Fascinating interspecies conflict, to be sure," Risa said with more than a touch of disdain. "But none of this helps the current problem at hand."

"No, it doesn't. It just makes things a lot more complicated," I said and took a step back.

Yilmaz appeared to deflate. The bravado was gone, and all that stood before me was a tired old woman.

"What did you tell the Jumjul?" I asked.

Yilmaz gestured at a chair, and I nodded permission. "That you were a part of a coup working to overthrow the Jumjul High Court."

"What?" Miles almost yelled. "You told them that?"

Yilmaz nodded and closed her eyes.

"But that wasn't on the charges you listed," Cain commented.

"No. I told them I needed more time to finish uncovering all the connections, to learn exactly which governments you were working for. It was easy to pin Miles to his brother and Cain to his mother. But the master?" She opened her eyes and gave an apologetic shrug. "That's a bit trickier. While the Glipglows might not be on the same level militarywise as the Jumjul, they're the major supplier of tech for the Jumjul. And once they latch onto something they like, they have a hard time switching it up."

"But why not just tell them the truth?" I asked. "If they know other governments are trying to move against them and side with the Eeri, then wouldn't everything we've learned be enough for them?"

"And confess what I've done? The illegal hacking with Project Clear Sight? Withholding valuable information? The development of the weapon Lucas used? Jumjul operate in black and white."

"Ah, right. I forgot that it's backward for someone like you. It's not the good of the many over the good of the one, but the other way around. So why would you put your neck out like that? It's not like we're talking about the continued future of the known worlds or anything," I snapped. "Why did you come here in the first place? To gloat?"

Yilmaz looked at me with weary eyes. "No. Your lawyers want to talk to you."

"That was… fast," I said with suspicion.

"The Jumjul have all the major law offices on standby. It's a standard part of how they operate."

"Fine, I want the call routed through here, assuming it can be?"

Yilmaz nodded. "I'll see to it."

She stood and gave me a long look before turning and leaving.

"That was…" Miles started but stopped and shook his head. "Did I really just see that? The commandant of the IGJ confessing?"

"Looks like it," I replied. *But did we? Or was it just another bluff? Would she really be at the end of her wits with all this?*

If the commandant would enjoy anything, I would've guessed it to be a good game of intrigue. But I wondered how many years of going through all that—the subterfuge, lies, manipulation—she could take before it wore her down.

Three high-pitched chimes sounded, followed by the long-held, low-pitched sound of a bell. A screen flared to life behind me, and when I turned, I saw none other than Harrison Bloodhearst.

21

The Love of a Father

"Ms. Orion." Harrison Bloodhearst was the eldest of the Bloodhearst brothers, and rumors had said he'd secluded himself away on Old Earth for years, leaving most of the business to his younger brothers and their hordes of sons and daughters.

"Hello," I said, a little unsure of protocol. When the message was delivered to me on the *Starshine*, that had been a recording. I hadn't ever talked face-to-face with an actual Bloodhearst in all my dealings with the law firm. "So, we've run into a bit of a difficult situation."

"So I gather," he said. "If you could make it brief… I'm due for my maintenance cycle in a few minutes. Let's see if we can get this cleared up for you, shall we?"

"Right. Um. So, first, I need to extend my policy. I'd like to cover a few others that are with me as—"

"I'm afraid I can't do that, Ms. Orion. Not if you want me to get the charges dismissed. I've been given the list of charges set against you, and I believe we can make a clear case of this rogue IGJ agent"—he seemed to read something off-screen—"one Mr. Turen ed-Suren, manipulating you in covering up his misconduct charges inside the IGJ."

"What?"

"It appears that Commandant Yilmaz personally sent out a memo stating Mr. Turen ed-Suren was no longer affiliated with the IGJ and was to be apprehended at all costs. She included you as a known associate, but I'm confident we can show the High Court a series of—"

"That's outrageous," I said. "Cain didn't do anything of the sort, and I can assure you, Mr. Bloodhearst, that he hasn't *manipulated* me at all. In fact, if it wasn't for him, I wouldn't—"

"Yes, yes. Fine. Perhaps we can cover him as well. But that's all, Ms. Orion." He leaned in a bit too close to whatever was projecting his image. Despite the life extensions I was confident he was sporting, they were struggling to do their job. "This is a most serious situation. I'm not sure you understand. The High Court will petition for your execution, not only because of the seriousness of the charges laid out against you but because of your association with your brother. The people across the known worlds need hope. They need to publicly see that the Jumjul are taking care of the situation when no one else is."

"That's not…" *Whoa. Do they even do public executions anymore?*

Miles stepped into view. "Excuse the intrusion, sir. I'm assuming you're aware of who I am."

Mr. Bloodhearst squinted and nodded. "Yes, of course. Your brother has already forewarned our office. If we engage in assisting you in any way, the emperor will discharge us as his lawyers."

"Fine. You know what?" I said. "Then forget it. I don't want your help. In fact, you can take me off your list of clients effective immediately."

The old man actually seemed to smile with relief. "If that is your wish, I will transmit the corresponding paperwork to the Jumjul. It might be a tad bit old-school, but we do still require everything to be in writing. Good day."

And with that, the screen went blank.

"What in the worlds did you just do?" Cain asked.

"If that old fool wasn't going to help all of us, then I don't need him," I said.

"Uh-huh," Miles muttered. "Remind me to up my insurance policies when this is all over. You're crazier than I am."

Maybe. But I wasn't just going to run out on everyone else, not after what we'd been through and how they'd stuck by me. "We'll find another way. We still have the Glipglows. If they get here in time, then maybe they'll give us sanctuary."

The master gave me a slight nod of encouragement.

"But in the meantime, I think we need to consider a jailbreak," I said.

Miles threw his hands up in the air and huffed. "From the Jumjul? Even I wouldn't try that."

"Sure you would, and you're going to," I replied.

Risa coughed slightly and said, "I'd like to talk with you. Privately."

"Alright. You guys put your heads together and figure

something out." When Cain scowled, I batted my eye-lashes at him. "Pretty please?"

<You're insufferable.>

<Yup.>

Risa and I stepped off to one side for a bit of privacy, as much as there was such a thing. The room had been constructed on a Jumjul scale, not human.

"I will help you get off this ship if you promise something in return," she said.

"And what would that be?"

"To do what your father should have."

I rocked back on my heels, trying to keep my surprise at bay. I'd been asking her about what had happened with Pops, and I was about to find out. "I'm listening."

"Wats was granted access to the Purified for one reason. His petition assured the Eeri he wanted to stop the Sun Worshipers, that if they succeeded, they would use what they gleaned from the Celestial Plain against the known worlds. That they were driven only by greed."

After a pause, Risa turned to gaze out the narrow slit of a window. "There was a price. Wats had to provide the Purified with genetic samples from the Sun Worshipers' databases, from everyone involved. But what your father didn't realize was that someone had added genetic samples from his wife and his children to the database."

I sucked in a sharp breath. *Oh, Pops. You really didn't know, did you, how truly special Mom's genetics were.* "And the Purified figured out my mom was actually an Error."

Risa leaned against the textured wall. "Yes. The Purified are paranoid after everything that happened even though it was such a long time ago. They have very long memories. And the Broken are their eyes and ears in the known worlds. They were aware of the Sun Worshipers and Wats. Nor was he the first to try to reach out to the Purified, a species which denies access to their world, to their culture and history. When you're hunting for an intergalactic mystery, that's like lighting up a signal flare and screaming that you have the answer."

I couldn't agree more, especially for humanity. We have an innate sense of curiosity, which often leads us into places we shouldn't go. But when a human is told something is off-limits or they shouldn't press the gigantic red button, they go right there or they press it. I know—I would've.

"But Wats was the first Sun Worshiper who agreed to allow the Purified access to the genetic databases. That was an opportunity to find more Errors, which the Purified would not ignore.

"If there's one thing that I've learned from the memories I carry, it's that Wats was a complicated man torn between two different philosophies. He grew up listening to the Sun Worshipers and their ideology, accepted it, and became one of them for years. But he wasn't without respect for the different cultures and species he came across in his work as a xenologist. He and your mother spent many long nights discussing the contradictions between the work he did and the system of belief he'd been raised in."

I squeezed my eyes shut and couldn't help leaking a few tears. After reading Pops's journals, I'd gotten a glimpse of the man who had truly been my father. And I was having it all confirmed.

"He loved her, your mother. And I believe he loved you and Lucas. And he came to reject a lot of what the Sun Worshipers believed, genetic purity among them. But he wanted to know what it was—more than anything—that he and so many had been working toward for so many years. And so he kept a secret. He promised the Purified he would destroy the work, killing all the people who promised to bring the Sun Worshipers one step closer to the truth of the Star Eaters. But there were two people he couldn't bring himself to kill, two people he hoped would carry on the work—not in some misguided attempt at glorifying humanity, but in order to carry on the work of a xenologist, to truly make contact with and understand those of the Celestial Plain."

"And so he killed those on board the *Rapscallion*," I whispered, "with the bacteria he was given by the Eeri."

Risa nodded. "The bacteria all Broken and all Purified carry within them. The bacteria is activated during the process of reclamation, destroying any genetic material that might allow the individual to fully connect with the Celestial Plain. But more than that, this bacteria can destroy those of the Celestial Plain. And that's where Wats betrayed us—betrayed us all, not just in sparing the lives of his two children, but in sparing the lives of the Celestial Plain."

At some point during the conversation, Cain had come over and wrapped his arms around me, and I leaned back against his chest. His warmth and presence provided comfort as my mind reeled. I'd put together the pieces on Epo-5, but Risa had provided the last little bits of information I'd been missing. And while I knew she could've been lying about it all, something inside me was telling me she spoke the truth.

"If the Broken carry these bacteria, what about Mahia?" Cain asked.

"She wasn't created within the Shell. She is an Error who has lived free of the Purified interference. She doesn't carry it."

I wrapped my arms over his and tried to burrow as deep as I could in his embrace. "If I had, then Mrs. Gol's plans to kill me wouldn't have worked. Remember?" I felt Cain nod. "But there's still one thing I don't understand," I said, turning my attention back to Risa. "How did Pops know about yo… I mean, my mom? That her genetics were the key?"

"I don't know if he did, not the complete story. Wats knew that the breeding program wasn't working, not as long as they maintained the idea of genetic purity. But there was something in your mother's genome which sparked his interest, something different." Risa's guard dropped, and she leaned forward to gently cup my face. "All you need to remember is that he loved her, deeply and truly. Genetic ideologies and research aside, he married her because he loved her. And I believe no matter what happened, that would've been enough for him."

Risa quietly moved away, giving Cain and me a moment of privacy. *<It's nice to hear confirmation of that. I'd always believed he loved her.>*

<I can imagine it is.>

<And as angry and confused as I've felt about learning the

truth about what he did, who he was, I… I can say that I think I understand. Not the purity crap but that need to know what exactly the Celestial Plain was. Not for power or fame or grand plans of making humanity the dominant species. Just the sheer bliss of discovering something different, something so completely foreign to you. Of having a whole new world and way of seeing the universe open up before you.>

<The heart of a true xenologist.>

<Yes. He really was, wasn't he?>

Cain tightened his grip and placed a gentle kiss on top of my forehead. *<And so is his daughter.>*

And for the first time since boarding the *Starshine*, I felt a twinge of pride at being the daughter of Wats Hawking Orion, a man who sacrificed everything in order to stop the Sun Worshipers from manipulating and using the Celestial Plain for their own purposes. He wasn't perfect by any means, and I was learning that no one was. No one was purely one thing or another, good or evil. We were a mixture of those two opposing forces every day, every moment, in every decision we made. And sometimes, individuals were forced to choose something hideous in order to try to create a path for something better in the future. Life was complicated and messy, and I didn't think I'd want it any other way.

"So, what are you going to do?" Cain asked.

That was a good question. I didn't know. The Star Eaters needed to be stopped from destroying any more worlds, and I wanted to understand why the Third had reverted back to using biological life as a fuel source instead of the sun. *Or are using both.* But I didn't want to destroy the Star Eaters. I wanted to figure out a way to help them find a way home. *But what will I do if we can't? Or if they don't want to or simply don't care or understand that what they're doing is wrong?*

"I'm not sure yet," I said. "I guess I'm going to hope that we'll find some other way to solve all of this."

"If there's anyone who can, I believe that's you," Cain said.

I gently pulled away. "Did you guys come up with any ideas?"

"Possibly, but you won't like it."

"Oh?" I said. "Let me guess—Miles's idea?"

Cain grimaced as though he'd tasted something sour. "Of course. But I think our chances would be better if we waited for the Glipglows."

We turned and joined the others. Miles had plopped down onto some squishy cushion that had ballooned up around him, almost as if it was trying to eat him. But he had a relaxed smile on his face, and even though his seat looked strange, I'd say he was quite comfortable. The master and Risa were quietly discussing genetics and biochemistry, technical terms and medical procedures that were way over my head.

"Alright, let's hear your idea, Miles," I said.

One eye popped open, then the other, followed by a languid stretch and a lazy grin. "Remember how the *Rapscallion* and its sister ships were built, with some of the specs mimicking Jumjul design?"

I frowned but nodded.

"I think we can all safely assume this isn't the brig but guest quarters. If we could get thrown in the brig, then we'd be a step closer to command."

"And your point? Jumjul security isn't going to be easy to break through. And any bioupgrades aren't going to be active. They won't be sloppy like that. Not to mention the little problem of Yilmaz. It's not like she's just going to stand back and do nothing. She's made it clear she needs to maintain a good standing with the Jumjul."

"Ah." Miles stretched again and pulled himself out of the squishy chair. "But you're forgetting one important thing."

"And what's that?"

"Us," the master said.

22

Deals within Deals

"Our talons carry adequate tech and would be in range to breach security. We are confident we would be able to gain access to basic command functions."

That seemed like a tall order, but Glipglow talons were notorious for their little tricks.

"And how do you know that would work?" I asked.

Miles waggled his eyebrows at me. "Didn't you hear what Yilmaz said? The Glipglows are major suppliers of tech for the Jumjul."

"And while I don't like this idea—" Cain said with a pointed look at Miles.

"You're just jealous I came up with it," he grumbled.

"And while I don't like this idea," Cain said a bit more loudly, over Miles's protest, "it's no different from how we worked together on the *Rapscallion*. Or when we were on Dar. You had knowledge of the tech they'd installed and used it against them. This time, it's the master who does."

A fair point. "And what about waiting for the Glipglows to arrive?"

The master gave two short rumbles then said, "Still a possibility, but we are concerned a ship hasn't arrived yet."

"And you'd rather wait for that?" I said, double-checking with Cain.

"It's by far the safer route. The Jumjul won't wait for the High Court if a jail break doesn't work," he said.

"Let me think," I told them.

So much was at stake that none of us could afford a misstep. But I was afraid we wouldn't be able to avoid mistakes. And besides, what was going to be our next move? If we broke free of the Jumjul, they would be hot on our trail. If we took refuge with the Glipglows *after* a jailbreak, no amount of concern over who supplied what was going to matter. The Jumjul would come after us in full force, and we would only back the Glipglows into a corner they didn't sign up for.

And where do we go from there? I needed to figure out how to get access to the Star Eaters, to talk with them and get them to stop so that we could all figure something else out. *And what of the Eeri?* I doubted things were going to calm down between them and the Broken anytime soon. *Are they upset enough about the fact I slipped out of their grasp that they would send the Broken still loyal to them after me? Or will they come after me themselves?* They had a powerful secret they would surely want to keep that way. The question was whether they would risk another war or push their allegiance with the Jumjul and drag them into everything. *And what of the emperor or the chancellor?*

I hated politics for this distinct reason. My head was pounding as I went round and round with so many possibilities, tangled alliances, and iffy motives. But only one thing really mattered at the moment, stopping the Star Eaters.

"Do we have any comms system in here?" I asked.

The master nodded and pointed at the window. "Refined smart glass. We can access the comm system for you."

Clever. I would never have guessed. "Alright. I want to talk with Yilmaz again."

"What?" Cain asked, a wave of suspicion flooding him. "What are you thinking?"

"I'm not sure, but I need to talk with her again," I said, keeping a tight lid on my emotions and thoughts. I really wasn't sure what I would say, and I didn't need to add any more arguments or theories into the already overwhelming mixture.

The master tapped on the glass with one of his talons. A cascade of colors appeared and settled into a slowly revolving mixture of hexagonal objects. No discernible writing was visible on the multihued screen, but the master didn't hesitate, and within the next few minutes, Yilmaz returned.

"Yes?" she asked. She didn't look as tired as she had before. *Perhaps confession was good for the soul after all.*

"We need to talk," I said. "You, Risa, and myself."

<What are you doing?>

<Just let me handle this. I want you guys to have your plan in place, just in case. As a backup only. Do you hear me? Backup only.> I thought the last words slowly and with emphasis. Cain's eyes darkened, and I hoped he was listening this time.

"Is there somewhere private we can talk?" I asked Yilmaz.

<Be careful, you foolish woman.>

<You too, grumpy.>

"If you insist, follow me," Yilmaz said.

Three Jumjul guards were waiting in the corridor and walked down the hallway with us into another room. It was fairly identical to the one we'd been placed in except it had a lot more of the squishy chairs. I tried one and sank down into the chair as it molded itself to my body, and I was pleased to find it was a bit warm. I leaned back and let out a long sigh of contentment. When I was comfortable and all tucked in, I looked at Yilmaz and was pleased to see her frowning. *Good. I want you slightly off balance.*

"Risa, you really must give these a try. They're quite comfortable."

Hesitant but following my lead, Risa settled into another squishy chair beside me. "Yilmaz?" I asked, gesturing at another one.

She shook her head. "I prefer to stand."

I shrugged. "Your loss, then."

"What do you want? Or was it just to get away from your overly protective groupies?" she asked.

I couldn't help but laugh. While trying to insult me, she was partly right. But I wasn't going to fault them for being overprotective. I was feeling the same way about them. And I felt good, having people who wanted to protect me and I them. That was a feeling I wanted to stick around for a long time.

"Risa and I are in the middle of making a deal, and

I wanted to know if you'd be interested in getting in on it," I said, all calm and cool. Even I wasn't sure where I was going with this, but I was following my gut, trying to channel a bit of the luck the universe had been throwing randomly at me.

"And what would that be?"

"She said she'd help us get out of here if I help her destroy the Star Eaters."

Yilmaz took me up on the offer—of sitting down. "That doesn't sound like anything new. I was under the impression that was already your goal."

"Destroy and stop are two very different words. But I'm guessing that this little change in nuance is much more to your liking."

"And if it is?" Yilmaz asked.

"Then we could use your help too." I leaned forward as much as I could in my silly seat. Maybe sitting in one hadn't been the best idea. *Channel your inner Miles.* I made a grand—and ridiculous—show of rearranging myself so that I could sit up a little taller. "I know how we can destroy the Star Eaters, but that's information we're going to keep to ourselves for the moment. I don't want you getting any ideas. But with the loss of your weapon—and good riddance, really—I'm betting you're scrambling, trying to figure out how to destroy the Star Eaters now. The Jumjul have a formidable arsenal. Perhaps you're considering something along those lines?"

The old tried-and-true Yilmaz shone through. "And what if I am?"

"I'll let you pin everything on me, not Cain or Miles or the Master. Not even Risa. But me, the last of the

Orions. But I want you to get us off this ship in *two* shuttles. If you're half as clever as I know you are, then you know I'll keep my end of this agreement. I don't want to see anyone else hurt, not because of the mistakes I've made. I'm willing to do what it takes to see this through. And I'll be the perfect scapegoat for the Jumjul, keeping you out of it. And I'll also be a handy piece of blackmail against the Eeri. If they don't want the worlds to know their hand in all of this, they'll keep quiet, too, and let me do what I need to."

A wry grin appeared on her face. "You are your father's daughter, after all."

"And so we have an agreement?" I asked.

Yilmaz stood up, and I followed suit. "I'll get you off the ship—all of you, I'm presuming?"

"Yes."

Her lips tightened with a brief pause. "Alright. I still have access to security systems as the Commandant of the IGJ. But if you don't hold up your end of the agreement… if the Star Eaters somehow make it through this, then your heart's blood and the little tagalong madman will be held accountable. Even the master. Is that clear?"

"Perfectly." I reached out, and we shook hands. When she tried to let go, I held on. "By the way, what happened to the escape pods from the *Samaritan*?"

"If you're asking if the Jumjul have imprisoned anyone else, you're wrong. There are no reports of any crew from the *Samaritan* being rescued."

I let go of her hand and bit down on my tongue to keep my emotions in check. "Before you return us to the other room, I need a moment in private with Risa, please."

Yilmaz frowned but nodded. When the doors closed, I turned to face her and put my thoughts on lockdown. Cain would be suspicious, but that was his tough luck.

"Not a word of this to the others," I told Risa. "What the others are going to know is that Yilmaz agreed to help us in return for our silence about how deeply she's involved."

Risa pushed herself out of her squishy chair—that was definitely its official name from then on. "How do you plan on doing that? Surely they're going to figure it out."

"Oh, I'm sure they will, but not until after we've gone our separate ways. When the time comes, I'll need your help to make sure Cain, Miles, and the master are in one shuttle, while we take the other one. What we need to do is for us alone. And if things go wrong, which they're guaranteed to do, I don't want any of them around. I want them safe."

"And you'll destroy the Star Eaters?" Risa questioned.

"I'll do everything in my power to make sure they don't continue," I said with a firm nod and a mental image of crossed fingers. Risa was clever, probably even more clever than I realized, considering how her genetics had been tinkered with. I highly doubted the Eeri created unobservant Broken to gather intel for them. I just hoped she wouldn't catch on until it was too late.

Yilmaz wasn't waiting for us, but we were escorted back to our original room by the Jumjul. Cain was standing by the narrow strip of glass, it having returned to its clear mode, and gazing out into the pitch black of space. When we entered, he barely turned his head, but Miles bounced to his feet and peppered me with questions.

"She's going to help us," I said for the fourth time. "She'll get us off this ship as long as we stay silent about her part in all of this. Nothing about Project Clear Sight or the weapon. Or her being a Gatekeeper. None of it. Are we clear?"

Miles grumbled a response, and the master nodded. Satisfied that I had at least a couple of minutes until Miles started churning out a new batch of questions, I went over to Cain.

"Aren't you curious?" I asked.

"No."

"Sulking, then?"

He looked at me, his eyes full-on emerald. "No. Just resigned to the fact that you make decisions that aren't always in your best interest."

"Cain, I—"

"Stop. I don't know what deal you really made with Yilmaz, but I can guess. And I'm also guessing you're developing a rather fatal case of hero syndrome, thinking whatever needs to be done, you can do it and keep the rest of us at arm's length."

<Dammit. I thought I'd kept my thoughts in check.>

"You did until now," Cain said with a wicked-looking grin.

I scowled. "Not fair, you know. But it doesn't change my mind."

"And I thought we said we were in this together." His voice was flat, and judging by the little black flecks in his eyes, he was barely keeping it together.

"We are. But I—" I spun around, unable to look him in the face. "After so many years of being on my own, of only having myself to rely on, having you—having Miles and the master and Lio and…"

His hands found mine and pulled me back around. "I understand," he whispered. "But you're not going anywhere without me."

I sniffed and gave him a small nod, but he lifted my chin up, forcing me to look at him. *<Is that clear, heart's blood? Where you go, I go. Live or die, this is together.>*

<But all I want is to keep you safe.>

<Don't you think I feel exactly the same way?>

He was right, of course. But my stubborn streak wasn't going to go away that easily. I didn't want Cain or anyone else to get hurt, especially not after losing Sam and Lio and Ochoa. *So many were on that ship, helping me.*

"Normally, I wouldn't intrude," Miles said softly.

"Yes, you would," Cain muttered.

"Fine, maybe I would, but I have something to say as well."

I pulled back and let Cain wrap an arm around my waist as we listened. Risa and the master had moved off to one side and were talking quietly.

"My life has been… an odd assortment of adventures, and that's putting it mildly. There were moments when I almost lost myself to the caricature I'd created after escaping my brother's prison," Miles said. "And for a time, I think I did. But working with you has helped me remember who I am. Not what I project out into the known worlds—the crazed would-be emperor—but the son of Old Earth, a man who yearned to bring his people into a new age full of partnerships, with arms open to the dozens of worlds and cultures out here. When we cut ourselves off from those we love and what we love, we risk becoming what we despise.

"I'm still not the good guy, as we've discussed before. I'm very much in the gray areas of life, but from that position, there are so many things I can do for good. Where others might have their hands tied, I can cross a few lines here and there. And I'm here for you, whatever you need, Mahia darling. If that means letting you go in your own direction so you can freely concentrate on what you need to do, then ask it of me. Or if you need me for something else, ask. But please, don't try to hide from me. Not me."

Tears were freely streaming down my face at that point, and I was a blubbering idiot.

The master had joined us by that point and gently wiped away a few tears, the rumble in his throat a comforting sound that I could feel reverberating in his touch. "Hatchlings have much to learn, and those of us who are privileged to care for them are honored by the growth they witness. You are a part of our den. And together, the den fights, lives, loves, and dies."

<Together.>

"Together," I whispered and wondered when the universe had given me the most wonderful gift of all—love, pure unconditional love.

23

Deadly Bargains

We hashed out a handful of different plans and eventually settled on one that wasn't as stupid as the rest. Risa, Cain, and I would take a shuttle and head for the Erith system. At the same time, Miles and the master would head for Glipglow space, looking for the ships the master was confident were out there. From there, the master would signal the den mother, and Miles would call in every marker he had. If I failed, the known worlds would need to be ready.

A day passed—that was my rough guess, at least—before Yilmaz appeared. Her skin was sallow, with dark circles forming under her eyes. When the door closed behind her, she stood staring at us for a few minutes before awkwardly clearing her throat. "Everything is in place. You'll be able to do what needs to be done. In thirty minutes, there will be a call to… service, I think, might be the right word—the one exploitable flaw in the Jumjul system. They have little fear of retaliation from species they don't consider much of a threat, and they adhere to a strict schedule of setting aside seven minutes each day to ponder the sacred mathematics.

"You'll have those seven minutes to get from here to the shuttle bay. I've timed it, and it should take you five minutes and thirteen seconds. The shuttles will be primed and ready to go. While the interfaces are basic, I've stripped what I could and dumbed it down to something"—she nodded at Cain and Miles—"you should be able to pilot. Get clear of the ship as fast as possible, then kick in your overdrive engines. The Jumjul won't follow."

She explained the route to us and made us repeat it back until she was satisfied. With one last look, she turned on her heel, but before she could leave, Cain stepped in her way.

"How do we know this isn't another double cross?" he asked.

At first, Yilmaz stood up straight, her shoulders thrown back, her head held high. But then she shifted slightly as though surrendering something. "You don't." And with that, she pushed her way past Cain and left.

"Well, isn't that comforting?" Miles said.

"It's what we've got to work with," I replied. "It'll have to work."

But those thirty minutes were some of the worst I've ever experienced. I paced back and forth, while Cain and Miles shared a few tense words here and there. Doubt filled my thoughts.

Just when I was about to seriously reconsider the whole stupid affair, Miles said, "It's time."

Our door opened, and the master ventured out first.

When the coast was clear, we raced to the shuttle bay. We didn't see a single Jumjul, and no alarm bells blasted. *A gamble that's paying off so far.* The shuttles Yilmaz provided were top-notch, the overdrive engines hot and ready to go. I still wasn't clear on what I was going to do in order to both stop the Star Eaters and try to help them, but I figured I could hash something out by the time we got there.

Cain stopped Miles and held out one hand. "You'd better live through this."

For once, Miles was speechless but grabbed Cain's hand then pulled him in for a hug. "You too."

As Cain darted toward our shuttle, I gave him a thumbs-up. He scowled and shook his head.

I looked back and noted Risa had leaned forward— *And is she giving the master a hug? What?* "Are you coming?" I asked, more out of shock than anything else.

She pulled back and said a few quiet words before running over to me and racing up into our shuttle. The master lifted an arm to wave then gave a small bow as he turned and went to join Miles.

"What was that?" I asked as we settled into our seats.

Cain took the pilot's chair, and I sat next to him, with Risa choosing to sit behind Cain.

"Nothing," Risa said. "He... he reminds me of Trax. That's all."

"Ready?" he asked, unable to keep the impatience out of his voice.

"Yes, let's get out of here."

Despite all my expectations that something would go wrong with my latest harebrained scheme, nothing did. Both shuttles launched, and we powered up the overdrive engines and were off.

"That was… unexpected," I said and let out a sigh of relief. "I was ready for Yilmaz to do something—"

"Hold on," Cain said, leaning forward and checking the console. "I'm picking up… No."

"What is it?" Risa asked, leaning forward.

"The Jumjul vessel—it's gone."

"Where did they go? Do you think she's trying to beat us to the Erith system? Or—"

Cain turned to me, his eyes wide. "No. Its codes are gone. As if the vessel was destroyed."

The comms crackled, and Miles's voice came through—not clearly but well enough to exhibit shock. "Are you guys reading the same thing? We're showing the Jumjul vessel doesn't exist. Do you think they've activated some type of shielding?"

"Sacrificing the many for the good of the one," I whispered.

"Come again? I can't quite make out what you said," Miles asked. "We're going to be out of range soon."

I cleared my voice and looked at Cain. "To sacrifice the many for the good of the one," I said, loud and clear.

"What's that… mean?"

"Miles? Come in," Cain requested.

But nothing was left but static.

"Surely you don't think that Yilmaz would sacrifice herself for… us, do you?" Cain asked.

"It's a basic tenet for those who practice the religion of the Seeds. That the needs of the one outweigh the needs of the many. Backward from what most might say, but…" I squeezed my eyes shut. Once more, so many lives lost because—

"Then we honor the sacrifice and complete our mission." Risa's voice cut through my growing sense of panic. "Yilmaz made her decision, and we've made ours."

She was right. We had a job to do. We would have time to grieve for all the lives lost, but right then wasn't it. *And if we don't make it through, then so be it.*

"How long until we reach the Erith system?" I asked.

"Two days and six hours," Cain replied. "We'll burn through the engines. Once we're there, we aren't going to be going anywhere. In fact, it's going to be tight the way it is. But Yilmaz…" His voice caught, then with a gruff cough, he continued, "Packed the shuttle well. We should make it. I'm assuming we're headed for Igridian Prime?"

"Yes."

"What if the Star Eaters move on by the time we get there?" Cain asked.

That was a question I'd been avoiding. All of this could've been for nothing.

"They won't," Risa spoke up.

I twisted around to look at her.

"It takes time. The process of harvesting is lengthy. At least, that's what the stories that have been passed down tell us."

"Then they'd better be right," I muttered.

We didn't have a lot to do on the shuttle. We listened to the news feeds and a few whisper nets but quickly turned them off. Everyone was panicking because no one felt they were being told the whole truth. Too many were speculating that the truth of the matter had been horribly obscured by alliances and back-door deals. Rogue groups were trying to take advantage of the chaos by taking military action against their governments and leaders. Crime rates were up, and IGJ agents were being pushed to the brink of what they could handle.

Cain forced me to eat, and while we were quietly munching on a rather bland ration pack designed more for a Jumjul palate than human, he broke the silence. "Tell us about the genetic memory. My understanding was that it was a Jumjul trait. I don't know of any other species who have disclosed that type of information."

Risa gave a long, drawn-out sigh before she answered. "You're correct. The idea was developed from the Purified's understanding of Jumjul genetics after they reached out with a Broken to gather information on whether the Purified wanted to try to establish a relationship with them.

"My understanding is limited, but from what I remember Trax discussing, the Purified realized the benefits of incorporating the idea of genetic memory into their Broken. Information instantly passed from one generation to the next, scaling back on time and effort. That also made the Broken dispensable. If one was killed or severely injured, another could easily be created to take their place. But if you're asking me about the scientific specifications, I can't assist you. That isn't a part of my training."

"Does this genetic memory extend to Mahia?" Cain asked. "Would she have inherited this from her biological mother? Or is it a part of the process of the Broken being created?"

"Where are you going with this?" I asked.

He shushed me. "Well, Risa?"

"That is a question I can't answer with certainty, only speculation. Mahia is an Error. She carries genetic material from the original Broken used to work with the Celestial Plain. But that was well before the Purified reached out to the Jumjul. I would be inclined to say no."

<*What's up?*> I asked him, still not following what he might be thinking.

<*Your visions.*>

"Oh," I said, the ignition switch in my brain finally firing. "You're thinking they might be memories and not real-time visions or communication?"

"It was a thought, but it doesn't sound likely," he said.

Risa leaned forward. "Visions?"

I felt a twinge of hesitancy at filling Risa in on everything I'd experienced, but I decided it was worth the risk. After I finished explaining what I'd seen and how I'd interacted with the Third, she looked shocked.

"What?" I asked.

"I've never heard any of the Broken describe such a thing."

"Not even on how they were all connected? The Star Eaters, the Third, or the Path Makers?"

"Not in how you've described it. But with the history I've been taught, I can begin to understand now." Risa leaned back and turned her head, a clear sign she was done talking.

<*Something I said?*> I half joked.

<*Remember, she may look human, but she is Eeri.*>

<*Well, isn't that just a cheerful little heads-up? Maybe you should've reminded me of that a lot earlier.*>

I was getting tired of admitting how often Cain made good points. But Risa—all the Broken—were Eeri, not in outward appearance, but intrinsically. They were no different from any species who had a wide diversity of subcultures. Humanity wasn't homogeneous by any means, but we had basic biological traits, core beliefs found in all the places humanity had settled amongst the known worlds. Remembering that Risa was Eeri—and knowing so very little about the species—was difficult. *And what part, exactly, is she going to play in all of this?* That question, I didn't have answers for.

24

Buying Time

As we reached the Erith system, Cain cut the overdrive engines. "Three hours with the main engines at max, and we'll be at the outer edge of the Erith system. There are six planets, one of which is in the Goldilocks zone, Igridian Prime. Another five hours, and we'll be at our target. Now is the time to fill me in on what you're thinking."

"We need to land on Igridian Prime. That's what I'm thinking," I said. *Land, and then I'll try to contact the Third. I'm just hoping I'll still be able to.*

"Hold on. Looks like we've got an incoming message," Cain said.

"Unidentified vessel, we order you to turn around. This system is under quarantine by the order of Chancellor Heron of the Aligned Worlds. Please be advised this system is under quarantine. You are being ordered to turn around."

"No surprise there," I muttered. "Shielding? Surely this shuttle has something we can use to slip by undetected."

Apprehension rippled through Cain, and before I could ask, he opened up a comms channel. "This is Turen ed-Suren Heron. Confirmation bio-ID alpha, seven, twenty-four, tango, thirty-three. I repeat, this is Turen ed-Suren Heron. Requesting a patch through to the chancellor."

"What are you doing?" Risa hissed.

"Following your lead, throwing caution to the wind," Cain replied ruefully. "We don't have time to play hide-and-seek. We need to get in and not worry about dodging any scout ships that might be about."

"Please repeat," a slightly anxious voice requested.

Cain did, and we didn't have long to wait.

"Turen?" a woman asked.

"Hello, Mother. Have the blockages lowered, and allow us access to Igridian Prime. There isn't time for a question-and-answer session. And if you hear from Zhu Akio, let him and anyone with him through as well."

"What you're requesting isn't—"

"I don't give a damn about your political game. You want to come out as the hero in all of this? Let us through. We'll take care of the Star Eaters. And if the emperor puts up any guff about his brother, you can tell him I know what he and his family did."

"What are you talking about?" Her voice turned sharp and full of suspicion. "Turen?"

"Just tell the emperor I know the story about his aunties. Now, let us through, or we'll punch our way through. Is that clear?"

After a moment of silence, another voice responded, "Unidentified shuttle, you are clear to proceed. Do you require—"

"No," said Cain.

<Thank you.>

<Yeah. You're welcome. But don't ever expect that we're going to family dinners or anything like that.>

Of course, Cain had to realize that, at some point, I was going to ask about the history between him and his mom. But I wisely stayed quiet on the matter—for the moment.

Whatever orders the chancellor gave, they worked. We passed through the Erith system with no more notifications. I was sure that we were being heavily monitored, though, and that the chancellor was working on figuring out what Cain knew about the emperor that she didn't. And if Cain's attitude was correct about his mother, I was sure she would use that heartbreaking truth to her advantage. I wouldn't blame her if she did.

"We're in range. I can bring up a visual of Igridian Prime," Cain said. "Do you want me to?"

Yes and no. Do I want to see the destruction the Third has done? Not really. But I needed to know what was going on, what we would head into.

"Do it."

He needed a few minutes to figure out the controls to pull up the image and manipulate it somewhat. But when he did, my heart sank. The picture wasn't one hundred percent clear, but it spoke volumes. Orbiting the planet was a fair number of abandoned ships and shuttles, many of them in pieces.

"Panic would have been instant and rampant," Cain said softly, "not only on the surface, but in space as well. They probably shot anyone trying to escape, fearing the spread of what they believed to be a biological contaminant."

"They aren't wrong," Risa said, anger in her words. "From what you've shared, the Third would've continued spreading even if it was off world."

I pushed back against my emotions, needing to stay focused. "We need a place to land—somewhere I can work, not risking you or compromising the shuttle. Can you do a scan and see if you can find a suitable location?"

Cain's brow furrowed, but he got to work. "I think the best bet would be to land in one of the heavily urbanized areas. This one"—he fiddled again and brought up a grainy image—"seems to have a space port. We could land there then make our way down through the city and out over… here. If I'm interpreting the shuttle's sensors even halfway correctly, I'd say this area seems to show a gigantic mass of the Third."

"Do it. We land there. But Cain, this time, stay with the shuttle. You can't come with us," I said.

<*No.*>

"Yes. And I'm not just trying to keep you safe. If things go horribly wrong, we might need a quick getaway. We land, let the shuttle cycle down. Even though the overdrive engines are shot, the primary engine still functions. Give it a chance to cool down, and if we need a quick exit, you can come and scoop us up," I reasoned.

Oh, he didn't like that and made me very much aware of what he thought of the idea, but in the end he gave in.

I twisted around to look at Risa. "And once we get to the Third, I make contact. Is that clear? Give me the chance to talk with them."

And another person was really unhappy with me. *Oh goodie.*

"We had a deal," she said.

"And we still do, but I want a chance to reason with them first. They listened to me before on Epo-5. Maybe they will again. Maybe we can find another way, one that doesn't involve any more killing—on either side." Then I sat up a little straighter and looked her dead in the eye. "But if that is going to be a deal breaker with you, then you'd better tell me now so we can hash it out… right here, right now."

"They need to be stopped," she said, leaning forward.

I wasn't sure I could take her in a physical fight, and I could sense Cain preparing to jump in if need be. Together, we would probably stand a chance.

"I agree. But there has to be another way. There are systems out there that don't support life. And if the Third and the Star Eaters can truly harvest the energy they need from the sun *without* the need for biological life, then we have to try. Give them a chance to go back home. But if they don't or won't, then we will do what we have to."

<I can put the shuttle on autopilot now. Location is locked in. I can restrain her if need be.>

<Do it and be ready. But only if we have to.>

I really didn't want to. I wanted her help. And I wanted to find a different way, one of negotiation and compromise. But the bacteria Risa was carrying was my failsafe. I had decided—if we couldn't get through to the Celestial Plain, then Risa would be the catalyst I needed to stop them. And yes, I fully understood what that meant I would have to do.

25

Second Chances

Risa remained quiet the rest of the way, and we landed on Igridian Prime with only a few bumps and bruises. I hadn't been aware of how much the Se Arkiathians had manipulated their weather. Without someone monitoring it, we had a few dicey moments in a runaway thunderstorm.

"Preparing to initiate the landing sequence," Cain said. "Everything still looks clear of the Third up here. Any idea how they find biological life? Some kind of sensory adaptation?"

"Nope. Not a clue. Just keep monitoring the area. If you have to take off, just continue monitoring from the air. But hopefully, you won't have to and can give the engines time to cool down."

<*And you had better be damn careful out there. Don't put up any barriers between us. Let me feel and hear everything. That way, I can come if you get into trouble. Clear?*>

I gave him a mock salute. <*Yes, sir.*>

With no regard for the close quarters, Cain reached

and pulled me to him. The kiss was passionate and heartbreaking.

<*Stay safe,*> I whispered. And before I could change my mind, I stood up and motioned to Risa. "Let's go."

I didn't bother to look for weapons. Anything we might find wouldn't help us against the Third. The sky was overcast, and the air smelled almost stale, but when a gust of wind kicked up, I caught the nauseating scent of decay. We didn't need suits or breathing apparatus. The Erith system had been a firm partner with Old Earth for centuries. The Se Arkiathians shared an eerily similar evolutionary pattern with humans, and while initial contact had been rocky—as it was most times—a trading partnership had quickly flourished and grown into a solid relationship. In fact, considering the Se Arkiathians as cousins of humanity wouldn't be that far out of line.

While Cloud-11 was the go-to spot for humanity's wealthiest, the Erith system had become the location for humans in the middle, with not enough credits to throw around on Cloud-11 but wealthy enough to afford a second home or split a vacation rental in this system.

Risa and I cautiously exited the shuttle and made our way to the edge of the landing platform. <*All clear so far.*>

<*Good. Slow and steady does it.*>

"Looks like the power is still up and running," Risa commented as an arrow lit up, pointing us toward a small lift.

"Might as well," I said with a shrug. "No sense wasting energy on trying to climb down."

We stepped into the lift, and a small screen flared

to life with a brightly smiling Se Arkiathian looking through us. "Welcome to Ke Korith, the unofficially five-star-rated shopping district for all your needs. Looking for the perfect retirement package? Or a relaxing getaway destination for you and your family? Look no further than the realtor market in the—"

I swiped my hand across the image, hoping to stop the ads, but up popped another face. This time was a middle-aged human woman, not as inviting as the first face. "Not finding what you're looking for? Stop at the Ke Korith information hub to browse through thousands of business listings. Sort and filter our compiled directory to find exactly what you need. Or if you prefer, ask one of our—"

I swiped again. The woman disappeared but was replaced by a strange-looking grub worm—I mean that literally—trying to sell a snack food I definitely had no interest in ever trying. "Damn ads," I mumbled and chose to just ignore them.

"Look," Risa said, obviously not bothered by the obnoxious music trying to get our attention and steal credits. She pointed at the building to our left. Across its bottom were thin tendrils of the Third. Some had wrapped around the once-stylish support pillars, while others had punctured windows and walls. As the lift gently touched the ground, I realized the Third had forced its way not only through the buildings, but through local inhabitants who hadn't been fast enough or willing to evacuate when they had the chance.

My stomach heaved, but I resisted. Seeing what the Third had done on Epo-5 had been an entirely different matter. Those had been skeletal remains, something one could examine with an easy dose of distance. But this was recent, gruesome and horrible to witness. *Do I really want to negotiate? Wouldn't it just be far easier and safer for everyone if we just destroyed the Celestial Plain? Most of the known worlds would hail us as heroes, provided they learned the truth of what was going on. Jupiter. Here I am, probably facing exactly the same ethical dilemma that Pops faced. How things always seem to come back around.* But I needed to be sure of myself because if I wasn't, I knew Risa would try to take advantage of the situation.

"You'll follow my lead," I said. "Clear?"

"Yes," she said with a touch of irritation.

"I want to make our way to the large mass of the Third that we spotted, then I'll try to make contact. We negotiate first." I stopped and turned to stare at her. "I'm not breaking my word. I am not my father."

She stared at me for what felt like ages, and I wondered what memories she might be recalling, memories that weren't hers but were still a part of her. *What exactly had Pops said? What promises had he made before appearing to have broken them? Will she just see the same thing, or will she be able to realize that I am different yet still his daughter?* I abruptly wished I had some type of weapon. It might not have done me any good against the Third, but it could've deterred Risa. *Foolish.*

<I can come, follow at a discreet distance. This shuttle appears to have remote voice capabilities,> Cain whispered softly. *<It also has targeting capabilities.>*

<And what if you get caught up in the Third? You wouldn't

be able to help then. No. Stay with the shuttle. Just be ready if I need you.>

<At the first sign of trouble…>

I appreciated his concern and willingness to do whatever it took. "Come on, we're wasting time."

I kept watching the Third, turning my head back and forth, looking for any sign of movement, some indication that it sensed us. But it didn't stir, nor did I see any dancing blue lights hovering around it, and I wondered what that meant. I understood so little about the Third and the Star Eaters. And even what I thought I knew had a strong possibility of being hogwash. Perhaps I was only projecting my human biases on a species that had no frame of reference for how I perceived the universe.

But the Eeri figured out how to communicate, even teaching them their language. So perhaps I wasn't too far off base with my theories. I tried to take comfort in that thought, but doing so was increasingly hard as we picked our way through the ruins of the city, a bustling metropolis only a handful of days earlier.

Just as in the space around the planet, the street was littered with debris. Broken transport vehicles, litter, and personal items were scattered about. I didn't want to, but I could picture the panic that must've raced through the city. At first, no one would've known what was going on as conflicting reports came in. But then images of the Third would have rolled in, making panic and disbelief erupt. The majority had probably tried to flee, racing for the spaceports or toward friends and family. A small majority wouldn't have believed anything, stubbornly refusing to leave or stop their jobs, thinking everything would just blow over. And of course, a curious few would've wanted to know, to see for themselves.

As we passed victims of the Third, I wondered which group each had been a part of. Those facing away from where the Third had erupted, I reasoned, had been trying to run. The looks of abject horror and arms outstretched for help that would never come were heartbreaking. But so were those facing the Third with equally terrified expressions as they realized their mistake. *Is that going to be me? Will I just wind up as food for the Third, my body slowly decomposing and—*

<Stop. That isn't helping, and you know it. Stay focused.>

I tried to clear my thoughts, but it was difficult. I couldn't help but imagine the screams of pain and fear that would've filled the now-quiet city as its citizens were consumed.

<Mahia,> Cain said gently. *<What happened here isn't your fault. You presented the Third and the Star Eaters a different choice. It was up to them to decide what to do, not you.>*

<But I should've—>

<This is not your fault. Say it.>

I couldn't.

<Say it, please.> His voice was gentle but still commanding.

Slowly, haltingly, I tried. But the words were broken, and I choked back my tears.

"Your father was a compassionate man," Risa said quietly, "but still tethered to a lifetime of indoctrination by the Sun Worshipers."

"He rejected the purity ideology, though. We've established that," I said, suddenly feeling a tad grumpy.

"Yes, he did. But the idea of completing what the group had been working toward for generations was compelling. He wanted to know. He wanted to understand the power behind the Celestial Plain. But you… you are different. I'm willing to admit that, even if I'm still skeptical about what you'll end up doing. Yet I believe you truly care about life, about how differences don't matter, about providing chances to do better, to be better."

I hadn't considered that angle, but it made sense. After Pops was arrested and splashed all over the news and whisper nets, all I'd wanted to do was prove that he wasn't the criminal everyone had made him out to be. I desperately wished that he'd been given a second chance and that people would do the same for me too. My last name being Orion didn't mean I was intrinsically bad or good. People should see me for who I was—not my name, but my actions, what I did, what I stood for.

"Thank you," I said.

We continued in silence, and the weight of the surrounding death wasn't as heavy anymore. But I looked at every individual killed, as we passed by, silently promising myself that my choices, my actions here, would show exactly who I was.

The tangled knots and webbing of the Third grew thicker as we headed out of the city. Our pace slowed considerably as we were both on high alert, watching for any indication the Third would come after us as well. But it didn't move, not even a twinge of awareness that something living and breathing was passing right by.

Then we saw it. A massive pillar of the Third had

burst out of the ground, twisted and turned into a shape reminiscent of a tree. *The capsa tree.* But its branches extended out across the wide expanse of the planet. If I hadn't been aware of the destruction the Third had caused, I could've admitted to seeing a sort of beauty in the scene. However, tangled up in its thick curving tendrils were many things once full of life: trees, plants, animals, and individuals, all pierced through or wrapped in the deadly embrace of the Third.

<Mahia? Can you hear me?>

<Yes. And we're here.>

<I just got a ping. Miles and everyone he could bring with him will be here in less than thirty minutes. He reports his weapons are hot and ready. And he's got a Zap 'n' Roll on standby as well, if need be. Whatever we need. And there's a bit of good news too.>

I sorely needed good news.

<The reason for the Glipglows being detained—they were picking up escape pods. Turns out there was a patrol ship not too far off the Samaritan's *position, and when they realized what had happened, they went to help rescue the survivors. When the Jumjul protested, the Glipglows threw a lot of addendums on their contract at them, forced the Jumjul to back off until they could figure out what was going on. Lio and Ochoa were among those rescued.>*

I couldn't help it. I cried tears of joy and relief. I'd wanted to hope they had survived yet hadn't wanted to risk my heart. But hearing they were alive was more than I had ever wanted.

<Thank you. I needed that. And tell Miles thanks too. I appreciate the options.> I sniffed and couldn't help but laugh and cry, and I tried to wipe away my tears.

"Cain says that—"

Risa held up a hand. "Quiet."

When I opened my mouth to question her, I caught movement out of the corner of my eye. The Third knew we were there. A tendril snaked out toward us—no, correction—toward me. I didn't move. This was what I wanted. I needed to make contact. And without thinking or letting myself get caught up in all the what-ifs, I bent down and extended a hand.

"Don't do anything rash," I pleaded with Risa. "The way the Third makes contact is going to look like it's trying to consume me, but if this works, it won't. I'll still be alive. You can monitor my biosigns. Please, give me a chance. Miles and the others are almost here. If I don't succeed, work with them to do what you need to."

Risa glanced up at the Third then back at me. "So be it."

I closed my eyes as the Third touched my hand, and I tried to picture the black sandy beach with the sea of light gently lapping at its shores. *It's me. Do you remember me? I helped you on Epo-5. We worked together there, and I'm hoping we can work together again.*

Something sharp pierced my hand, then I felt something else pierce the middle of my back. I could feel every move the Third made as it dug through my skin and spread inside me. I opened my eyes. "Remember. Wait. Give us a chance."

Who knows what Risa had expected to see, but her eyes were wide, and her face had turned pale.

"Give us a chance," I whispered one more time as my world slowly went dark.

26

Don't Ever Make Assumptions

I remained completely aware in the darkness. The faint sounds of trash being pushed around by the breeze. The sharp intake of breath from Risa. The sensation of the Third winding its way through my body and wrapping around my spinal cord. But the pain was gone, replaced by warmth and, dare I say, a comforting sensation.

Then gradually, the darkness rose, and I was once again standing on the Celestial Plain.

The ocean of sunlight was calm, and after a few steps forward, my toes were at the edge. I dug my feet into the warm black sand and turned my gaze to the dark sky, a thousand glittering stars stretching out before me. The sand shifted to my right and moved to once more mimic my form. Bright-blue lights twinkled beneath its dark skin, and it stood there with me, staring out into the endless expanse of light.

"I thought we'd come to an agreement," I said. "I helped you join with the Star Eaters to take the light they harvest and feed that to the Path Makers. Why have you come here and killed this planet?" I could've been softer and subtler, but we were running out of time, and that really wasn't my style.

My lookalike slowly turned to face me, the sand along its face shifting into a distorted Ray of Oblivion. It reminded me of a sand garden where someone was endlessly trying to draw the Ray but erasing it and starting over, again and again.

"What does that mean? Did something else go wrong?"

The half-formed ray disappeared, and another one tried to form. This time, the Ray of Ascension. Then it, too, was wiped away, and the Ray of Confluence appeared.

I shook my head. "I don't understand. Is there a different way we can communicate? Can I talk with the Star Eaters? Can they come here? I've been able to talk with them before."

Even without a basic understanding of the creature standing before me, I sensed its growing panic and dismay. The rays appeared, half formed, one after the other, until I caught sight of something different. Something else was buried beneath the sand, something pale… something trying to escape.

The lookalike's head flung back, and sand poured off it, the pale interior slowly being revealed until I was staring at Pops. I jumped, stumbling back a few steps. When I looked again, it wasn't Pops, it was Risa. No, that wasn't right. The face *shifted* in front of me, features rearranging, taking on a different shape, until it settled on its last form.

"Hey there, big sis."

"No, that's not possible. I stopped you. Defeated you," I said, stepping back again. Lucas or what looked like him stepped forward, and I scrambled to get out of his way.

"Defeat me? Did you really think it was that easy?"

"Yes." I swallowed, racking my brains for the memory of what had happened. *The Third had wrapped itself around him like a large net. It had tightened and constricted.* And so I had assumed Lucas had died and the Third had consumed the life within him, as it had so many others. Then Yilmaz went after us, and we scrambled to get off the planet. And we'd never gone back to make sure. *Idiot. A damned idiot.*

"So, what happened then? I'm all ears," I said, forcing myself to stand my ground as the initial shock was wearing off.

Lucas lifted a hand, wiggling his fingers and turning it back and forth. "I almost died. Nearly. But we are Orions, after all. We've got a sneaky way of figuring out how to survive."

"That tells me nothing," I said.

He grinned. "The Third tried to consume me. Oh, it killed my physical body, but since I was connected in a much different manner than other life-forms, my… shall we say energy or life force was preserved, kept safe in this place. I know you don't ascribe too much to the soul"—he paused and looked thoughtful—"unless I missed something during all those years apart. But the Third and I joined, the ultimate ascension, I think you could say. And now, I've finally completed what generations before us weren't able to do. I'll take humanity into its next golden age as we travel from galaxy to galaxy, multiplying and—"

"Save it. I'm not here for the sales pitch."

No matter what had happened to him, the good old Lucas was still in there. He didn't like being interrupted in his moment of glory.

"I'd rather know more about what's happened to you. How long did it take? What did it feel like?"

"Ah, ever the curious little xenologist. Just like good old Pops, eh?" Lucas said. "Fine. Let me explain what you weren't good enough to do."

That's it, just keep on talking, you puffed-up little ego monster.

<Cain? Can you hear me?> I didn't know if I could communicate with him like this or not, but I had to try.

<Mahia? How? I brought the shuttle over when I sensed the Third. I can see you, and I don't like what the shuttle's readouts are telling me.>

<Cain, I've got a sneaking suspicion of how to end all of this. But you're not going to like it.>

I felt him hesitate, then I realized he already knew. *Poor man.*

<Is there any other way?>

<No.>

"All this time, we held the genetic key everyone was looking for. If only Mrs. Gol had paid more attention to what Pops was doing. Triton, you and I, my children… we all could've been the first. Together, we could've taken the known worlds by storm, destroyed those who wouldn't follow, and together, spread our family legacy to the rest of the universe. We would've been hailed as…"

I zoned out again. *<Lucas is here. And if he's here, then he's manipulating the Third. And that means if we're going to give the Star Eaters and the rest of the Celestial Plain a chance, then I need to stay here too.>*

<What do you need?>

<Keep an eye on Risa. Give me a chance. But if it doesn't work, then——>

<I understand.>

I wanted to say so much more. Or to return to my physical body and give him one last hug. But none of those were options. I turned my attention back to Lucas, who had grown silent and was watching me. *Whoops.*

"Whatcha thinking, sis?" he asked carefully.

"Oh, just considering the dozen different ways I'm going to stop you. That's all," I replied casually. I needed to be careful. If Lucas got even a whiff of what I was up to, then all bets were off.

He laughed again. "Really? You think you've got what it takes?" His laughter turned ugly and visceral.

The Third erupted out of the black sand, its tendrils formed to razor-edge points. They swayed back and forth in an invisible breeze—or perhaps to the demented music rattling around in Lucas's head. He'd always had awful taste in music. But those sharpened edges glinted in the light from the stars above us, and as they danced, they crept closer and closer. I took a step back until I felt twin needles of pain in my shoulder blades. I twisted around and saw the beach was covered in the snakelike tendrils of the Third. I had nowhere to run.

"So, what? You're going to kill me? Is that it?" I asked.

"No. If I killed you, then you would share in my

glory. And we can't have that, now can we? No, we're going to keep your body alive but your mind trapped here, helpless and unable to do a damned thing about it." He leaned forward, his eyes turning into that black sand with blue lights buried in their depths. "But I'll let you watch," he whispered.

He straightened up, and the Third nearest to me moved with lightning speed, wrapping around me until I was good and stuck. Then Lucas waved a hand, and the sand at my feet glimmered then morphed until it was a grainy representation of Igridian Prime.

"Neat trick," I managed to say. *<Cain, you and Risa need to back off. Lucas can see me. He can't know that you guys are there. Hurry!>*

"Isn't it, though?" Lucas said with a wicked grin. He waved his hand again, and the image on the ground zoomed in to show where the Third had taken hold of me. I would've sworn my heart stopped beating for a minute or two as I looked desperately at what Lucas was showing me. But I couldn't see Risa or Cain.

"Did you really think that you alone could stop me? I mean come on, sis. Even I knew I needed help. I worked hard to find those who would be loyal to me at any cost. What did you do? Think you'd be all heroic and stuff and come here on your own? Where's that little half-breed of yours? Hmm?" Lucas taunted.

But his insult didn't faze me. Instead, I got stuck on what he was implying. *He still thinks I'm alone. Maybe I've got a chance after all.* I tried my best to put on a terrified face as I looked down at the image he was showing me. *But could Lucas really not know?*

Or… the Third. I'd been brought here, and it wasn't Lucas initially greeting me. The Third had been trying to tell me something. Perhaps Lucas wasn't as strong as he thought he was.

"All settled in and comfortable?" Lucas asked as I kept quiet.

I chose not to respond. I wanted to keep him off balance, and the best way to do that was to ignore him. He'd never enjoyed being ignored.

"No pithy remarks? No insults for your little brother? Or how about begging for mercy?" He closed his fist, and the Third tightened its grip around my body. "I could grant that, you know. Let you go here and there. It'd be short-lived. This planet won't last much longer. In fact, I don't think the system will, actually."

Okay, so much for ignoring him. "Are you controlling them too?" I asked.

Lucas frowned. "Who?"

"The Star Eaters, dummy," I snapped. "They're out there, sucking the sun dry."

A fleeting look of emptiness crossed his face before arrogance snapped back into place. *Hmm. He definitely doesn't have the control he thinks he does.*

"Once we've gathered enough energy to fuel the last of the Path Makers, we will take our rightful place in the universe." He turned away and stared out across the sea.

<Mahia. Hold on a little longer. Let us get into position first.>

<We? Cain? What's going on?>

I glanced down and didn't see that anything had changed. I was there, held within the deadly embrace of the Third, but no one else was around. Cain had said he'd taken the shuttle, but whatever he was doing, he wasn't responding. And right then, neither was Lucas. *Perhaps my question about the Star Eaters spooked him.*

The sand shifted next to a grainy image of my physical body, moving as if a serpentine creature lay underneath its surface. I didn't want to make any sudden movements that might bring Lucas's attention back to me, so I tried to watch it out of the corner of my eye. A thin tendril of the Third poked up out of the sand and seemed to hesitate for a moment. But then it snaked forward and wrapped around a part of the Third holding me.

I'm here. I'm willing to help. Please. My time on Epo-5 had proven the Third wasn't one complete collective. It could be influenced and make decisions on different fronts. I had no idea what that actually meant, only that I still had a chance if one part of the Third agreed with me and not Lucas.

Ascension. Unity. Sacrifice. The words were whispered in my mind, and I knew they weren't from Cain.

Did something go wrong with the Ray of Ascension?

"Unity. Sacrifice. Death."

Three words were hardly anything to go on. Each one could be interpreted in a hundred different ways, but I'd already been arrogant enough to believe I understood what the Third had wanted from me before, with such cryptic remarks. *Why should now be any different?*

"I'm getting a tad bit hungry," I said.

Lucas didn't move.

"Hey, you. My idiotic brother. I'm talking to you."

That got his attention.

"I'm hungry. Got anything to eat around here?"

He had the audacity to roll his eyes at me. "What do you want?"

"For you to snap out of your little meditation session over there and get on with it. If you're going to finish all this, then just do it. I really don't have any interest in watching you gloat."

"Really? Are you sure you're ready? There isn't any coming back from this. Not this time."

"I'm sure. If you're going to lead humanity off the edge of the cliff, I'd rather not join. Thank you very much."

Lucas squatted in front of me, the window into the physical world gone.

<Cain, I love you.>

I wriggled and tried to move, testing my bonds one last time, but the Third didn't budge. In fact, I would've sworn it got a tad bit tighter. With Lucas controlling most of the Third in this space, I didn't stand a chance. I was only going to make a difference one way. In order to attain unity, I had to make the ultimate sacrifice. I had to die. Again.

"You know what? Just do it," I hissed. "I'm done being an Orion—only a bunch of messed-up Sun Worshipers hell-bent on destroying the known worlds. Why would you think I'd want to stick around?"

For a moment, I would've sworn Pops's eyes were staring back at me. Lucas resembled Pops so much that looking at him hurt. Tears rolled down my cheeks.

"You've won," I whispered. "You were right. I was never like you. I could never have done what you've done."

Lucas reached out and touched my cheek, wiping away a tear with his thumb. "Now there's something we can agree on." And with nothing else, he stood up and backed off as his part of the Third moved, filling in the gaps, trapping me in that place. But that one small sliver of the Third not aligned with Lucas was also there, waiting for its chance.

Now. I'm ready.

"Unity. Sacrifice. Death," it whispered repeatedly as it snaked up my torso, weaving in and out of its brethren until it found what it was seeking. I closed my eyes and waited for the pain to come as the Third pierced my heart.

27

Sacrifice. Unity. Life.

I opened my eyes and noted I was still in the Celestial Plain. Something was different. Lucas wasn't anywhere to be seen, and I was free of the Third. Taking stock of my surroundings, I noted that something was *beyond* the black beaches.

Not really worrying about anything else—like what I'd just let Lucas do and what Cain was going through—I made my way across the beach. At the edge wasn't land, exactly. I knelt and dipped a hand into what I could only describe as blue lava—not a very adequate description, itself. I'd seen vids of vulcanologists working with techs and engineers on terraforming projects. Before I applied to work at Whimsical Heights, I'd briefly considered a few companies, like Atom Adam's Liquidation and Hydration, which was a ridiculous name for one of the top-rated terraforming groups out there. But after all the traveling I'd done with Pops, I'd wanted to settle down where I could just keep my head down and mind my own business. Too much media attention surrounded companies like that, from the top CEOs to the kitchen staff.

Everyone wanted to know what the next great project was going to be—or what would fail. Everyone loves a good public failure too. And I'd had enough of that.

But I'd done my research, and I had really enjoyed the vid series on vulcanologists.

While it certainly looked like lava, it didn't burn off my nonexistent hand. It felt warm, and that was all. I stood and, with a shrug, took a step. I sank a few centimeters into the warm substance, so I took another step—still didn't sink. As I slowly walked across my strange new discovery, I noticed that about a meter in front of me, the lava was bubbling. Curious, I took a few more steps and watched.

Then I realized. *Slow on the uptake, Mahia.* This was the Third, and from its strange embrace rose a Star Eater. No robe hid its glory, nor did any of the Third stick to its surface. It was glorious to behold, a shining beacon of light shifting into different shapes until it settled on a distinctly humanoid form. From behind it rose the second Star Eater, and off in the distance were Path Makers, all slowly making their way out of the Third.

"So this is what you really are?" I asked.

The Star Eater closest to me shifted again, and it chose the face of my pops. But that didn't bother me. In fact, I found it rather comforting.

A reply came, but I never saw its mouth move. Instead, I *felt* the response echo within me. Intuitively, my brain took those feelings and translated them. *This certainly would've been handy from the start.*

"We are of the Celestial Light, the last. Our home— our galaxy—died before yours was born, and we have traveled, always seeking, always hoping to find a suitable galaxy, a place where we can rebuild upon the Celestial Plain."

Oh. Alrighty then. "But something went wrong when you came to my galaxy, right? That is what the Third tried to show me."

After a flutter of confusion, it gave the sensation of relaxing. "Yes. The Third. Our Great Gatherer and Caretaker." The Star Eater turned and gestured toward the great blue expanse. "We have traveled only a few times. The energy required is heavy upon those of the Celestial Plain, and when we came to your galaxy, we were frightened and asked our great Path Makers to move too soon. This caused a tear across the fabric of what unifies the Celestial Plain, at a level of destruction we were unprepared for."

"Why were you afraid?" I asked, urgently praying that no great monster was chasing them. I really needed a break, even if that meant chilling for eternity in this place.

"We were three before we traveled," the Star Eater said. "And then we were two."

While I was relieved, I also felt a wave of sorrow. "That's… I'm sorry."

"But now we can be three once more," the Star Eater said, extending a hand toward me.

"What?"

"You have sacrificed in order to defeat the corruption. We do not take this gesture lightly. You have joined with those of the Celestial Plain, and we invite you to join us and to become one with those of the Celestial Light."

"I'm… honored. And slightly speechless. But I think before anything like that happens, we should deal with Lucas—the corruption, you so aptly named him."

"Yes. The corruption must be purged before we have consumed the last of the light from this star. To travel with the corruption was a risk we accepted, hoping in a new galaxy strength could be renewed to defeat the corruption. But with you, there may still be time."

"Then how do we stop him?"

The second Star Eater had joined us. "We will provide you with the unity necessary to battle and purge our Great Gatherers of the corruption."

They reached out and touched my forehead before I could ask another question, like practical information or a how-to manual on what needed to be done. Light flooded my brain, literally—nothing but a brilliant, blinding light.

When I blinked, the Star Eaters were gone, and off in the distance was Lucas. Huge webs of the Third shifted all around him.

Right. We'll figure this out as we go. Nothing new there.

"Hey! Little brother… guess who's back!" I yelled.

Even at a distance, Lucas was startled to hear me and see me confidently striding toward him.

"Guess what? I got invited to the party you always dreamed of going to," I said.

I'm going to assume you're with me? The sand trembled at my feet, and I smiled viciously. I was going to enjoy this.

"That's not possible!" Lucas yelled and stormed toward me. "I trapped you here. You're under my authority now. How are you—"

"You know what? I'm done with our little chitchats." I pushed my arms forward, fingers splayed wide, and my Third erupted out of the ground. *Go get him.*

The gesture was probably a bit overly dramatic, but it felt good. My Third raced toward Lucas and his Third, the two halves of the Great Gatherer entangling each other. I could feel every strand of my Third as it struggled, working to wind its way around the other and gain supremacy. And we were winning. The power I felt thrumming through me was intoxicating, and I pushed at the Third, watching it grow and overpower Lucas.

I walked up to him and leered. "Your stupid little purity shit show is over."

When I raised a hand, ready to destroy him, he laughed. A new wall of the Third erupted up behind me and fell down around me before I even had a chance to react. It sliced and chopped at my Third and at my body. Where it stuck, my flesh bled away into shining drops of light.

"Whatever you think you've done, you haven't," Lucas said as he got back to his feet. "I'm the master here. I know how to manipulate and bend the Third to my will." Then he crumbled into a million different pieces of sand and reformed into a monstrous vision of the Third.

"Sacrifice. Unity. Life."

The words echoed in my head. *Gotcha.* Then I let go of any preconceived notion of what my mind or my body was in this place. Light poured out all around me, and I spun it into tendrils of my own, whipping myself at Lucas. Where he touched me, I merely shifted, healing and reforming myself into a thousand different shapes. But where I touched him, he crumbled, the pieces of Third burning and smoking.

And I knew what I had to do. *Come to me. As much as you are able. Join with me, and together we will purge ourselves of the corruption.* I could sense them, all of them. The Great Gatherer, moving through the sandy beaches, joined with me as I spun them into something new, something different. And when I knew all who could answer my call had come, I looked at Lucas.

I'm sorry, little brother. I truly am. But there isn't a place for you here. I can only hope that in whatever comes next, you find some peace.

We exploded into a supernova. Our light flooded the Celestial Plain, burning through every single piece of Lucas and the Third he'd manipulated until nothing was left.

This time, I was sure he was gone. I had destroyed my brother. I had finally won.

28

To Be an Orion

We expanded out along the dark beach and joined with the other two Star Eaters. It was bliss. Pure peace and our awareness stretched out beyond the system we were in, beyond all the planetary systems and the sun within our galaxy. So much life was out there, endless possibilities being created and destroyed over and over again.

"Unity."

The word slid through the peace, and we felt it: wholeness, completeness, and pure unity. No corruption. Nothing broken. Celestial Light. The Great Gatherers and Caretakers. The Path Makers. All reunited. All one.

Then we sensed something *wrong*. Something was out of place that shouldn't have been there. And the *wrong* thing hurt.

The peace we'd felt was ripped away, and we were torn apart, forced to exist with separate awarenesses. And another was trying to join us, to break through into the Celestial Plain.

We formed the dark sandy beach in our thoughts, the endless sea of light and the tendrils of the Great

Gatherer wrapped around the bodies we chose to represent ourselves.

There, another mind, another presence. I reached out and shaped the mind, forming it and bringing it with us onto the Celestial Plain.

"Who are you?" I asked.

Another living thing appeared before me, eyes wide and wild. Its face felt familiar, a face constructed of flesh, of the beings here in this galaxy.

"Mahia?" it asked.

Am I? That was a name I had once been called.

"Who are you?" I repeated.

It stood, dusting itself off and looking around. "Are we…? Is this what you talked about? With your visions?"

I felt the concern from the two behind me. *"Is this another threat, so soon after we've found unity?"*

"We are of the Celestial Plain," I said.

It turned, its eyes focusing on me. "We? You're Mahia Orion, a human. Or rather, mostly human. You don't belong here."

I felt a twinge of confusion. Of course I belonged there. This was unity. We were of the Celestial Plain.

It stepped forward and reached out a hand. "Don't you recognize me? It's Risa."

Risa. The name sounded familiar, as though I'd used it in another time and place. But as I gazed upon the creature before me, the name wasn't what I recalled, but the face.

"Mother?"

A look of concern formed on its face but quickly

passed. "Yes. I'm your mother. Mahia, it's me. What are you doing? I thought we had an agreement."

I tried to respond, but a wave of pain washed over me, and I felt my light dim.

"What's wrong?" the creature asked.

"Something isn't right. Something is destroying the unity," I whispered.

"Ah. Yes, that would be me."

I looked at the creature in shock. It wore a face I was drawn to, one I knew had brought me love and comfort in another place and another time.

"Why would you hurt us?" I asked.

"We didn't know what was happening. Nothing changed. The Star Eaters haven't stopped. Miles is saying we haven't got much time before we won't be able to get to a safe distance from this system. Whatever you were going to do, it didn't work."

"But the corruption is gone," I said. "We purged the Celestial Plain of its corruption. We are going to find a new home, a home where we can find life once again, renew and continue our unity."

The creature I called mother frowned and looked beyond me at the two behind us. "You're going to have to explain. And do it quickly."

Another wave of pain rushed through me, and I felt myself diminish. The tendrils of the Great Gatherer and Caretaker were shrinking back into the safety of the sands.

"Mahia, whatever is going on, you've got to snap out of it," the creature said. "Tell me what happened."

Something awoke inside me, and I looked at the creature. "Risa? What... what are you doing here?"

"Shells of purity, focus, Mahia. What happened!"

"I... Lucas. He had... He was the one controlling most of the Third. I thought we'd destroyed him on Epo-5, but somehow, he had..." The words were hard to bring back, but I tried. "Completed unity. But he was the corruption. I..."

The other Star Eaters stepped up on either side of me, each one gently touching a part of me, helping me sort through the jumble of emotions, words, and images. "Our unity had been corrupted. Now our unity has been restored. We offered the gift of the Celestial Plain to this life who sacrificed itself so that we may live," we said as one.

"But you're destroying this system," Risa snapped. "You're just going to do what you did before."

"No," I said, trying to clear the haze. "No. I mean yes. They need the energy from the sun, but they want to move on, to find a new galaxy, one where they can thrive without harming others. These are all that remain of the Celestial Light. They deserve a chance to start over."

"Deserve?" she asked.

The Star Eaters dropped their hands, and I felt my light diminish and flow back toward them, leaving me vulnerable and alone. But my mind was crystal clear.

"Risa," I said, this time knowing for sure who I was talking to. "How in the worlds are you here?"

"I'm like you, remember? Or, rather, like your mom. I can join with the Third. With a bit of help, that is."

"What?" I asked.

"But you need to tell me straight. Did you hold up your end of our deal?"

"Yes, I did. I stopped Lucas. The Third won't go after biological life again. The Ray of Ascension has been fulfilled, for real this time. No corruption left." Then I realized. "Wait, if you're here, then that means… The bacteria. Risa!"

"Yes, I know. That's why we don't have much time. Can you assure me that they are leaving our galaxy? For good? That they're not going to destroy any more planets or suns? This is the only system that they need in order to leave?"

"Yes," the two Star Eaters said. "You have our word."

"Mahia?"

"Yes. It's true. But what does it matter anymore? If you're here, then that means the bacteria is already working its way through the Third," I snarled. "You lied. You went ahead and—"

"No. I didn't. But you… died. And we needed to know what was happening. This was the only way."

"The only way for what? To make sure you've killed the Celestial Plain? Taken away their choice at being able to move on and leave us in peace?"

"No. Think, Mahia. You were infected with the bacteria as well at one point. What happened?"

"I almost died," I snapped. "Wait. I *almost* died. But the master…" A huge grin split my face. "You sneaky little cloud sucker. That's what you were talking to the master about."

Risa nodded. "Yes. A contingency plan. You just need

to tell me how to wake up so the master can deliver the cure. They worked on something a little larger in scale than what they did for you, enough to make sure they could protect the Third if the time came."

I didn't think about it or if it would even work in that place, but I leaped forward and pulled Risa in for a hug. "Thank you."

"Don't thank me yet. I need to wake up and tell them."

"Oh, right. About that…"

"A Vow of Assistance can be formed." The Star Eaters then turned toward me. "As the Vow of Unity remains between us."

"Mahia?" Risa asked.

"They're all that's left. Just these two. Their species… or life form, was dying. It's just the two of them, the last two of the Celestial Light."

"And what about Cain?"

Pain burned in my chest at hearing his name, pain that had nothing to do with the bacteria slowly making its way through the Third. "I hope he understands," I whispered quietly.

"He might, in time, but right now…" Risa trailed off. She didn't need to say it.

"Just tell him that I'm sorry and that I love him. That I did all this in order to help them, to stand up for what was right, no matter the cost." *Exactly what I had believed my Pops had done.*

"The choice is yours," the Star Eaters said.

"Yeah. To melt away into nothingness or go with you on the adventure of a lifetime," I said.

"Is that her only choice?" Risa asked, addressing the Star Eaters. "Or could you… bring her back? Restore her as she was somehow?"

Dummy. Why didn't I think to ask that question?

"This is possible," the Star Eaters said.

Something brushed against my feet, and I looked down at a small tendril of the Third. It wound its way up my leg and snaked across my belly until it was long enough to pull away and—I would've sworn—look at me.

"Unity. Sacrifice. Life."

"You would do this?" I asked.

"Unity. Sacrifice. Life."

"Yes," the Star Eaters said. "Do you wish it?"

"But what about you?"

"We will still have unity. We will continue on."

"Then yes, please. Yes," I said.

"Then wake," they said, and Risa vanished. "The Celestial Plain thanks you."

I blinked, and when I opened my eyes, I was back on Igridian Prime.

"Mahia! Oh gods, if you ever do anything like that again, I'll kill you myself," Cain said as he grabbed me and about squeezed me to death.

Shocked, I blubbered like an idiot for a few minutes before realizing I needed to check on Risa. "Let go, you big oaf. Where's Risa?"

<*I love you too, by the way,*> I added.

"I'm here," someone said in a sleepy-sounding voice. Risa was over to my right and wrapped up in the Third with the master standing over her.

"We've provided the antidote, and it should take effect shortly, but there have been some unforeseen consequences," the master said with a worried snap of their lower jaws.

"It won't work, will it?" I asked, suddenly feeling the crushing weight of doing all this for no reason.

"No, it will work. The master has assured me of that. But… because the bacteria is unique to my physiology, because I was a genetic recreation by the Purified… I won't survive without the bacteria," Risa calmly said.

"But—"

"No. This is my fulfillment of my oath, that the Broken would one day stop the Star Eaters. I understand it means the Star Eaters will journey on, but from what you've said and shared with me, I truly don't think they mean any harm. And I'm hoping they'll extend the same offer to me that they did to you. And perhaps, wherever they go, if we encounter life again, I can help them find suns without worlds supporting life. Perhaps we could find a place where the Celestial Plain can coexist while harming nothing else."

"Do you understand what that means?" I asked.

She nodded as her words became more slurred. "Yes. I do. More than you probably realize. I've discovered my place. My purpose. And I thank you."

Her eyelids slipped closed, and I knelt down next to her, gently reaching out and placing a hand over hers. "I wish we could've had more time together," I whispered. "Thank you for believing in me."

My hand tingled, and soft blue lights appeared at my fingertips, gradually spreading across my fingers and up my arms.

"Mahia?" Cain asked.

"Nothing to be worried about. I got a little parting gift is all. Actually, more like a party trick, probably," I said, trying to joke.

We stayed there until Risa stopped breathing, and even then, I didn't want to go.

<Come on. We need to go.>

<I know. It's just…> I looked down at the face of my mom, at the face of Risa. And I saw my Pops and even Lucas in there too, the whole Orion family. As mixed up as we had been, with widely different motivations, in the end, it was an Orion who helped save those of the Celestial Plain. It was an Orion who'd worked to help save a life form so totally different from our own. I was proud to be an Orion. And I knew Pops would be proud too.

29

The Last Unexpected Guest

Miles had brought more than a few of his friends. He'd brought an entire fleet of ships, supported from across the known worlds. Once we were all safely tucked away on the *Snapdragon* and far enough away from the Erith system, we sat down, and each shared their experiences. The master profusely apologized for their deception, and I reassured them we wouldn't have survived without their intuition in helping Risa. I had no idea how to really thank the Glipglows for helping out the survivors from the *Samaritan*, but the master assured me it was the den mother's honor to be able to assist.

Our little crew gathered in Miles's quarters, a hearty meal spread out on the table. We listened to the news feeds as we ate, quietly adding our own personal experiences to what was being reported. The chancellor, the emperor—who was speaking right then—and the new commandant of the IGJ were spinning a story of a major radioactive meltdown on Igridian Prime, which had been run by the Sun Worshipers and not the Star Eater cult. They told lie after lie about going in and destroying the last of the Sun Worshipers and their base, regretting the tremendous loss of life but assuring the masses that their sacrifice was necessary in order to protect the rest of the known worlds. The Erith system was now officially off-limits. Anyone who crossed the border that the IGJ were setting up would be shot on sight.

I couldn't help but wonder exactly how long that would last.

"So, they patched you up, then?" I asked Lio.

He glanced over at Ochoa. "Yes. More or less. The Glipglows have an amazing array of technology. But I fear there will be some things that will never fully heal."

No more than that needed to be said. I completely understood. What I'd seen the Third do on Igridian Prime would haunt my dreams for the rest of my life. And while I knew everything had worked out more or less for the better, I couldn't help but feel the weight of all of those lives lost.

<You won't carry that burden alone.>

I looked over at Cain and smiled. No, I wouldn't. I let my eyes sweep across the table, glancing at each person. We'd gone through this grand adventure together, and we all knew the truth of what had really happened. But the sense of belonging I'd gained wasn't just about having people to share that with, to help carry the load of the memories and the sacrifices, it was also about the friendship and unconditional trust and love we all shared with each other.

An officer's voice came over the comms. "Excuse me. We have a shuttle requesting permission to dock."

"ID?" Miles asked, already pushing his chair back.

A ripple of tension flowed through us.

"It's a fake ID, sir. We're not entirely sure who it is, but they're insisting that they be allowed to come on board."

Miles looked at me, and I shrugged. Cain shook his head.

"Let them through, but I want security there to greet them. Be ready for anything. It's not like we've made a bunch of friends out there," Miles said. "You coming?"

"Of course. Why should you have all the fun?" Cain said.

As all of us headed for the shuttle bay, I couldn't help but spin through a whole list of suspects. *The IGJ? The Commandant would know what really happened if he truly read through those files Yilmaz had.* But if they were going to use us as scapegoats, I would've expected our names to have already been blasted across the media.

"Let security go in first," Miles said. "Get the real ID, then we deal with them."

We agreed, except for Ochoa, who insisted on going in with the security detail. Soon, she returned with a sly grin. "Cain, Mahia, if you'll come with me, please."

<Know what's going on?> I asked.

He shook his head, but if Ochoa wasn't concerned, then I wasn't going to be either.

As we stepped through the doors, an alto voice rang out loud and clear. "Turen."

Chancellor Heron.

Cain froze.

<Go on.> I nudged him.

But he didn't move.

<It's just your mother, silly.>

He turned, his eyes liquid emerald as he stared at me. *<You don't know her like I do.>*

<Then introduce me.>

"I take it you've found your heart's blood?" she asked as she approached, or glided, rather. Her dark-auburn hair was streaked with deep hues of violet and arranged artfully in a bun on top of her head. Someone had added little gems that twinkled in the light as she moved. The dress was long and tailored to fit her body like a glove, its deep purple accentuated with bold splashes of blues and greens. She shared the same cranial ridges that Cain had, but as far as I could tell, she didn't sport a tail. *Interesting.*

"Well?" she said, eyebrows arched. "Have you forgotten all of your manners?"

Cain coughed and gave her a small bow. "No, of course not. Mother, let me introduce you to Mahia Orion… my heart's blood."

She turned and looked me over—really looked me over, not even trying to be polite about it either. "It is a pleasure to meet you."

"Pleasure to meet you too," I said with my own little bow. "What brings you here?"

"As much as it is nice to see my son after all these years, I came here for the truth. I'd like to know what really took place and why"—she turned and looked at Miles, who'd followed us—"your brother is an idiot."

If I'd had a mouthful of water, I would've spat it all over her. That was definitely not something I expected to hear from someone like the chancellor.

Even Miles looked shocked, and Cain started laughing.

"Are you okay?" I whispered.

He nodded. "Yes. Fine. Miles?"

Miles shrugged, still looking shocked.

"Mahia?" Cain asked. "Just know that whatever we tell her, she will eventually twist it to her own advantage."

Chancellor Heron narrowed her eyes but gave Cain an approving nod. "If necessary, yes."

<Then perhaps not quite all of it,> I said.

<I'll let you decide what to say and what not.>

The whole situation was awkward, and I left out several things, but I did share what we knew about the Eeri and the Broken. I was fairly sure we would see repercussions from what had happened on the Eeri home world. The chancellor agreed, even remarking that rumors of a civil war were already forming. But she took our explanations without complaint and, once we were finished, asked to share a few private words with her son as he escorted her back to the shuttle bay.

"What do you think that's all about?" I asked Miles as we waited for Cain to return.

"Not sure, but I can bet she's asking him to come home, probably take up some kind of office or something," he said.

"You don't think he will, do you?" I asked, a bit of anxiety rising in my chest.

"Seriously? You have to ask me that? Can you imagine Cain as a politician?"

No, not really. Good grief. I really hope not.

When Cain returned, he wasn't happy. She had asked him to come home, it turned out, but he refused, and the age-old issues between them had ignited once more. He didn't tell me much, and I didn't press. I knew that when he was ready, he would share.

According to the ship's internal clock, it was almost time for the second shift to go off duty, and Lio and Ochoa made their excuses, citing they wanted to catch some sleep before they went on duty. Both had recommitted themselves to Miles's service, and I suspected that Miles was going to find Lio another ship to captain and that Ochoa would be his chief of security.

"Sleep tight. Don't let the dermatex bite," I joked.

As Lio chuckled, Ochoa paused for a moment. "I plan on it, and I don't want to hear about any more adventures from the pair of you for a while. We all need a break, got it?" she said with a slight twinkle in her eye.

"Got it." I laughed.

The master stayed with Miles, Cain, and me for quite some time, happily listening to Cain and Miles share stories of when they were younger and far more stupid. But eventually, the master stood and said they'd made arrangements with one of their ships to take them back to the Glipglow home world.

"After all that we have experienced, we have a wealth

of information and research to attend to. But remember that you are a part of our den, and you are welcome to join us whenever you need. In fact, we would consider it an honor if you would visit us. Share in our den at some point."

"We will, I promise," I said, and I meant it. That was an honor above honors and one I wasn't going to miss out on.

As the door closed behind the master, Miles looked over at me and grinned. "Cake?"

"You read my mind," I said, matching his childish exuberance.

We stuffed ourselves on the sugary goodness until we couldn't eat any more. We were spread out on Miles's couches. I was lying down, my head resting in Cain's lap, and Miles was sprawled out on the couch opposite ours. "What are you going to do now?" I asked.

"Oh, I've still got my hand in all sorts of things. There's always something to work on. Plus, I might pay a visit to my brother. There are a few things that I think need to be put straight. Mind you, I don't have any ambition for the throne. You get more done in the shadows anyway. But humanity needs to reset its objectives, make sure we get the last of the Sun Worshipers and get rid of their purist ideology crap."

"I think that would suit you," I said. "Maybe I won't think of you so much as a madman, but the shadow man."

Miles considered it then smiled. "I think I like that. The Shadow Man of Old Earth. Maybe I'll unofficially officially make that into a title or something." He yawned and stretched. "I don't know about the two of you, but I think I'm ready to fall asleep for the next three years."

<I'm ready for a bit more than sleep,> Cain said.

I shot up and headed for the door. "No problem. See you, then."

Miles laughed as Cain followed me. "Sleep, you two. You need sleep. But when you're… rested, come and see me. We'll talk. I have a few ideas for the two of you as well. After a well-earned break, of course."

"Of course," Cain said with a slight swish of his tail.

As we headed back to our own quarters, I took Cain's hand. "I don't know about working for Miles," he said. "That could get… complicated."

I shrugged. "I'm not too worried about it right now. We can decide where we go, what we want to do. I've still got a shipload of credits."

"Enough we could buy our own ship?" he asked.

"Probably three or four, to be honest," I replied. "Why?"

"I like the idea of just the two of us going off and traveling. Exploring. Even though I worked with the IGJ, I didn't get a chance to see much more than wherever I was stationed at the time. I'd like to explore." He paused. "If you're up for that, that is. I would understand if you've had too much of exploration and—"

I laughed. "No, I think that sounds just right. But first, we're going to stop at the Lunar History Zoo."

Thank you for coming on this grand adventure with Mahia and Cain, and reading *The Celestial Light*!

There will be more coming in the Embedded Universe with new faces and some familiar places, so please stay tuned!

If you want to explore my other titles, or make sure to stay up to date with what's happening, visit my website and sign-up for the newsletter!

elizabethknollston.com

You can also follow me on social media at:
facebook.com/elizabethknollston
twitter.com/EKnollston

Thanks again for going on this journey with me and all the crazy characters in my imagination!

Acknowledgements

It's hard to believe I'm wrapping up my fifth book, and the final one in this series. I'm forever grateful for my parents who encouraged me to read and explore the magic contained within a book. I'm so grateful to them and how they always celebrated my unique outlooks and passions in life.

This series wouldn't be where it is today without all of the fantastic editors from Red Adept Editing. I've appreciated all of their hard work, their great feedback, and all the work they did to help these books shine. Thank you so much!!

A huge thank you goes to Naomi who has been on this author journey with me for several years. Without her support and wisdom, I would still just be daydreaming about being an author. And another round of thanks goes to Katie who has helped bounce ideas around for these characters and been a huge cheerleader with this series.

My family has been so supportive of this adventure, I have to say another huge thank you to them. They've listened to my fears, my excitement, sat through conversations where I've doubted myself and always been there to reassure me. They've listened to my wild ideas, helped inspire characters, and been some of my first readers.

And of course, a huge thank you to all of my readers for taking a chance on these books. I'm so grateful for each one of you, with your kind words of reviews and encouragement. I hope to bring you more stories of far-off adventures!

About the Author

Elizabeth Knollston collects dragons. No, they're not real. But if you know of a mad scientist or genetic engineer who's working on the real deal, be sure to let her know. She would dearly love to collect star ships too, but those won't fit in her garage.

Her (overactive) imagination is credit to her parents, who outrageously encouraged her poor spending habits of buying too many books. And just a side note—if you ever plan on moving, book collecting isn't helpful.

In another life, Elizabeth dreamed of becoming an archaeologist, but a fascinating and rewarding job as a therapeutic horseback riding instructor derailed those plans. When Elizabeth isn't wondering about being on a manned mission to Mars, she enjoys bugging her dog, battling the weeds in her garden, and being a productive member of society.